Praise for

Keeper of the Kingdom

"Aimed at young adults, this is ingenious enough to appeal powerfully to adults who wonder how far this entire computer age can go. And that ending . . . —is brilliant. A compelling read from exciting beginning to just as exciting ending." – *The Book Reader*

"Kids will be drawn into this timely sci-fi adventure about a boy who mysteriously becomes a character in his own computer game. The intriguing plot and growing suspense will hold their attention all the way through to the book's provocative ending." – Carol Dengle, *Dallas Public Library*

"This zoom-paced sci-fi adventure, set in the kingdom of Zaul, is a literary version of every kid's dream of a computer game. *Keeper of the Kingdom* may be touted for youngsters from 9 to 13, but I'll bet you my Spiderman ring that it will be a "sleeper" for adults as well." — Johanna M. Brewer, *Plano Star Courier*

"A must read for children interested in computers and computer games. From the first page to the last there is no relief from the suspense and tension. H.J. Ralles has found a way to connect computer-literate children to reading." — JoAn Martin, *Review of Texas Books*

"This is an excellent story and I was very pleased with the storytelling. I would recommend this book to young adults who are not only into computers and computer games but are also into science fiction." — Conan Tigard, *BookBrowser.com*

Visit author H.J. Ralles at her website

www.hjralles.com

To Colby,
Happy Reading!
H. J. Ralles

Keeper of the Kingdom

By

H. J. Ralles

Top Publications, Ltd. Co.
Dallas, Texas

Keeper of the Kingdom

A Top Publications Paperback

Fifth Printing December 2005
12221 Merit Drive, Suite 950
Dallas, Texas 75251

ISBN#: 1-929976-03-8
Library of Congress # 00-135779

Cover Design by William Manchee

The characters and events in this novel are fictional and created out of the imagination of the author. Certain real locations and institutions are mentioned, but the characters and events depicted are entirely fictional.

Printed in the United States of America

For my sons,
Richard and Edward
with love

Acknowledgments

Malcolm, my husband and best friend, for your never-ending support;
Lynn Rae Kastle, for your tremendous editing and friendship;
Sally Fallis, for reading the first draft and offering reassurance;
Laura Hart of Motophoto, Plano, for terrific publicity photographs;
Joe Chicoskie, Barbara Reed and Brenda Quinn–your comments and
encouragement helped me realize my dream. Now it is your turn.

Chapter 1

"**H**alt, intruder! In the name of Zaul, the Protectors command you to surrender!"

Matt ignored the warning and continued to run. A vibrant blue ball of light flashed past his head. He fell to the ground and covered his ears as the shimmering sphere of Xeleron struck the wall and exploded with an almighty boom. The stench of burning chemicals filled the air. Tiny fragments of plaster rained down as if he were in the middle of a sandstorm. Matt could taste the dust on his tongue and feel bits of debris tangled in his hair.

Two Cybergon Protectors were visible in the distance; the fine silver barrels of their Xelerays were aimed straight at him. A direct hit would mean instant death.

Matt struggled to his feet and carried on, his life depended upon it. The walls of the corridor flashed by as he frantically searched for a way out.

"Halt, we command! You will not escape the Protectors. Surrender or be eliminated!"

A second ball streaked past, made contact with the floor twenty feet ahead and detonated. Using his personal computer, Matt shielded his face from splintered fragments of tile, which hurled through the air towards him. A sharp pain seared through the back of his hand. Gasping in agony, he pulled a jagged piece of floor tile from his flesh. A long crack now wound its way across the lid of his laptop.

The dust settled. An enormous blackened crater, still sizzling from the intense heat, blocked the way forward.

"How do I get out of here? Someone help me please!" Matt cried. But in this ghastly place there was no one to hear.   Breathing heavily Matt battled to his feet again. His eyes fell on an exit to his right. He dove through the archway as the ceiling behind him exploded. The force of the blast sent him spinning across the cold floor tiles. Out in the corridor, debris fell to the floor in chunks, blocking where he had just entered. A cloud of dust surged inwards stinging his eyes and attacking his lungs. He picked himself off the floor, coughing violently. The pile of rubble would delay the Protectors and give him vital extra minutes.

Masking his eyes from the bright sun, which pierced through an enormous transparent domed roof, Matt staggered further into the hall. He turned quickly in circles to survey his surroundings, shaking with fear as the awful reality dawned on him.

"Nowhere to hide, there's nowhere to hide. Gotta find somewhere quick," he muttered in a daze.

Everything was unfamiliar, a strange mixture of primitive and yet very advanced technology. Silver ceiling pipes wrapped their way through the roofing beams. Strange white grids broke the monotony of the deep red floor tiles. There were no windows, a single closed door, and a staircase barely visible at the far end.

Can't keep running, he thought. *Gotta try and outsmart them.*

His eyes desperately scanned the stark white walls and dozens of angular steel pillars, which supported the elegant glass roof. He hated heights but the clever way out was up. Matt staggered towards an enormous pillar in the center of the hall. It was a woven mesh of thin metal struts spiraling towards the ceiling, an ideal climbing frame. Above, a broad steel girder linked one side of the hall with the other. It would make an excellent hiding place, but could he reach the top before the Protectors broke through?

The back of Matt's hand throbbed. The cut from the flying debris was deep. Blood stained his jeans in large red patches where he had pressed his hand against his thigh to control the bleeding. Climbing with his personal computer would not be easy, especially with an injured hand. Matt quickly pried open the top studs of his denim jacket and placed the black computer inside, firmly fastening it afterwards. The jacket waistband was fairly tight; he would have to risk it slipping out.

There was no time to waste assessing his options. Already he could hear voices in the corridor and the movement of the fallen concrete. The Cybergon Protectors were ruthless and were not easy to out-run. With no human emotions and a programmed purpose, they would pursue a target until the end. They were closing in on him.

Matt shoved the toes of his Nikes into the latticework and began the climb. The steel edges of the pillar were cold and smooth. It looked a long way to the top.

The smell of his sweat was strong and he could taste the salty perspiration forming above his upper lip. His right hand felt numb.

Keep going, you're doing fine. Don't look down, he told himself over and over, as he grappled with his fear of heights.

His shirt stuck to his back. The heat of the sun's rays bore down upon him through the glass dome. Every inch he climbed felt as though it would be his last. He fought back the tears.

The clammy fingers of his left hand finally curled over the edge of the steel girder. They slid as he attempted to haul himself onto the beam. Matt grabbed the girder with his weakened right hand and attempted to lift his left arm over the top. In the endeavor he lost his footing. For an awful heart-wrenching moment his legs dangled in the air. Using every ounce of remaining strength, Matt hauled himself on top and disappeared from view just as the Protectors entered the hall.

The Cybergons clambered over the rubble and walked resolutely toward the center of the room. Matt pressed his body flat against the steel girder, hardly daring to breathe as the footsteps stopped abruptly beneath him. His heart pounded against his chest cavity. *Surely,* he thought, *this is some kind of nightmare?*

The sharp corners of Matt's personal computer dug into the base of his ribs. He gripped the beam tightly ignoring the discomfort and found the courage to look over the edge. The height was dizzying.

Two Protectors stood directly below. Tight navy suits

covered with numerous protective plates hid their robotic forms. They were indistinguishable from one another except for the large gold numbers stamped on their sleeves and across the front of their metallic helmets. Penetrating purple eyes glared through a narrow slit. Matt shuddered.

"The intruder has escaped us," said Protector 21, disarming his Xeleray, and pointing it at the stairs.

"Commander Z will not be pleased," said Protector 34.

"Then we must find him."

"Agreed. He cannot get far; he has no where to hide," said 34. "The workers will not help him. They know the punishment for hiding a fugitive."

"We must notify the other units of a security breach immediately."

The shiny silver weapons hung loosely by their sides. The Xeleray was unlike anything Matt had seen before. Long and thin with a large viewing sight on the top, the weapons seemed weightless as they swung by the Protectors' thighs, yet he had already witnessed their destructive capabilities.

A third set of boots entered the room. They walked more lightly and at a quicker pace. The tall human figure adjusted his tailored purple jacket as he approached the two Cybergons standing in the center. Only a wide mouth and pointed nose were visible through openings in a silver fabric hood. The man's eyes were concealed behind a dark rectangular band of Acrylic Sheet. Displayed on the sleeves were several gold stripes, indicating a superior rank.

"Commander Z, we have no further news of the

intruder," reported Protector 21. "We assume he took the stairs to the lower level."

"I am not impressed, 21," shouted the Commander. "How can you let a boy elude you?"

"He cannot get far, Commander, Sir," said Protector 21.

"That is no excuse for your incompetence," replied Commander Z in an agitated tone. "I presume that you have informed all other Protector Units of the security breach?"

"Protector 34 was about to key in the alert, Commander, Sir," said 21.

"Then do it quickly, 34!" snapped Commander Z. "Before the intruder manages to leave this sector completely."

Protector 34, was one of thousands of programmed Cybergons under the control of twenty-six human Commanders. He walked towards the far side of the hall where a concealed door opened in the wall, revealing a small computer terminal. From above, Matt watched an image appear on the large rectangular screen.

Protector 34 began his conversation. "Contacting all Protector Units. Commander Z requires you to be on Red Alert. We have a young male intruder. No further description available at this time."

Matt suddenly felt very ill. His eyes focused on the deep cut across the back of his hand, which tightly gripped the edge of the steel girder on which he lay. He watched in horror as a thin line of blood trickled over his knuckles and splattered in fine drops on the floor in front of Commander Z's boots.

"Is the intruder a Worker or a Liberator?" Commander Z asked Protector 21.

"Unknown at this time, Commander, Sir," 21 replied.

"Exits must be closely monitored, 21."

"Agreed, Commander, Sir."

"We must catch the intruder and make an example of him. All Workers must see what will happen if they attempt to escape the Kingdom of Zaul and join the Liberators," said Commander Z with authority. "The last thing I want is a rebellion on my hands!"

Further drops of blood fell to the floor. Matt could only watch and pray that the color would not be noticeable on the red stone tiles. He dare not alter his precarious position for fear of losing his balance. Another trickle rolled to the edge of Matt's hand and down to his knuckles. *No, please, please, don't fall,* he thought.

Protector 34 called across the hall to the Commander. "All Units now on full alert, Sir."

The Commander's attention was temporarily diverted. He turned to acknowledge the Protector's report.

"Very good, 34."

"The identity of our intruder must be determined, Commander," said Protector 21.

"Agreed. We will start with a roll call of all Workers. The Keeper will expect a full account of this incident. "

The blood fell to the ground as the Commander walked away. Matt felt a wave of relief flood over his body.

Commander Z and Protector 21 joined 34 on the far side of the hall. The three figures stood together on a series of green floor tiles adjacent to the computer terminal.

A red light flashed on the screen and the floor began to vibrate. Matt's deep blue eyes widened as he witnessed Commander Z and the two Cybergon Protectors slowly disappear from the vast hallway.

It was some minutes later that Matt found the courage to move. *I can do this, I **can** do it,* he told himself firmly. He slowly shuffled backwards until he could feel the steel pillar at his feet. His legs shook violently with the shock of all that he had endured. Matt had never been particularly athletic, and today's events would have tested even the physically fit. He knew that his ordeal was far from over.

Slowly Matt retraced his steps, trying not to look at the ground as he descended. He had climbed at least thirty feet and finding a foothold was not easy. Matt reached the halfway point. He clung to the metal struts and took a breather. The concealed entrances used by the Protectors worried him. He wondered how many other hidden doors the computer terminals would open and if vibrations always preceded their use. Would he be aware of the arrival of anyone else in the hall before it was too late for him to take cover? His legs felt like rubber when they finally hit the ground.

It took Matt a few seconds to compose himself. The computer screen on the far wall was now blank, and any attempt to use the Protector's System would be futile without knowledge of the exact computer entry. To pass through a concealed door without awareness of what lay on the other side could be fatal. Might he be able to clamber through the gap in the rubble and retrace his route?

No, the Protectors would surely be sent to repair the damage to the corridor, he thought. *The staircase is my only option.*

Looking only ahead, he clutched the computer still tucked in his jacket and ran as fast as he could across the hall. Matt reached for the handrail, his lungs aching, his breath coming in gasps.

The steps spiraled steeply downward. It was impossible to see in the low light how far they went, and visibility faded with every step. After the brightness of the hall above, it took his eyes some time to adjust to the change in light. The steps were concrete, and it was very difficult to descend quietly. He listened for the sound of anyone coming upwards.

The carpeted corridor at the bottom was dimly lit with small yellow lights spaced several feet apart down the center of the ceiling. The starkness of the white walls and metal pillars of the level above was now replaced with a dark eerie atmosphere, which was even less inviting. He still had no idea in which direction he should head to find an exit and avoid further confrontation with Protectors. A hum of machinery could be heard in the distance to his right and so it seemed the obvious choice.

The pungent smell of chemicals grew stronger. At the end of the corridor two steel doors prevented Matt from continuing. He hesitated, wondering if it would be stupid to walk blindly through into the unknown. A dark alcove to the right contained yet another wall-mounted terminal.

Matt's curiosity got the better of him. He could not resist the challenge of an unknown computer. He placed his good hand on the keyboard and lightly fingered the round plastic keys. Unlike his laptop, there were no recognizable letters facing him, but a strange array of symbols.

The huge doors suddenly opened. Matt sprung away from the keyboard and moved towards the back of the alcove in panic. Three Humans in dark baggy coveralls heaved a heavy trolley through the open door. A body lay motionless on the top, covered with a white linen sheet. Matt noticed a limp arm hanging down. One person was weeping quietly.

A Protector suddenly appeared in the doorway. He threateningly waved his Xeleray at them.

"Hurry to the Disposal Room. You still have another four hours work. The time will be added to your day."

"Yes Protector 13," they mumbled in unison.

Protector 13 tapped his Xeleray, studied the trolley for a few minutes, and walked back inside. The heavy doors swung closed.

The trolley squeaked as it was wheeled along the corridor. Matt followed closely behind in the shadows. The three figures silently pushed the load past the base of the stairs and into a small doorless room on the right. Matt peered round the open entrance to witness the removal of the sheet. A young woman wept over a pale and lifeless body of a boy, which lay on top of the trolley. She stroked his forehead tenderly.

"Is Targon still alive?" she asked the others.

"Barely, Dana, but I think we may have fooled Protector 13 this time. We have to get the boy to see Dorin fast."

"Can you carry him, Balder?" Dana asked.

"Sure, but you and Norak will have to cover for me. Protector 13 will not accept my absence for very long," Balder answered.

"Dorin works the night shift, so you should find him in his room. It's the ideal time for this to happen," said Norak, running his fingers thoughtfully through his blonde hair.

"Return the trolley and pretend that the boy has been disposed of. Take the ID tag from around Targon's neck as proof of his death, and tell Protector 13 that I had to visit the Cleanliness room," said Balder. "Now hurry or this won't work."

"Good luck Balder," Dana and Norak said. They quickly wheeled the metal trolley back out of the room and into the corridor. There in front of them stood the frightened figure of a boy dressed unlike any of their own kind.

Chapter 2

Dana gasped. "Who are you?" She studied Matt's denim clothing and backed away. It was a child for sure, but not one of them.

"Please help me," Matt stuttered.

His hand continued to bleed periodically. Weak from his experiences, and relieved that he had finally found a friendly face, Matt stumbled and grabbed the edge of the wall for support. Dana saw his genuine distress. Her caring instincts took over from her uncertainty.

"You poor child, you look terrified, and look at your hand! Come in here, quick!"

She flashed a glance each way down the corridor and grabbed Matt by the shoulders, pulling him inside the small room.

"Sit on the floor and let me have a look at that cut."

Matt found the gentleness of her touch soothing after the horrors he had witnessed. Looking over her shoulder, his eyes fell on several large black doors on each of the three facing walls. The heat was unbearable. He knew that he was looking at furnaces used to cremate the dead.

The more he saw of this world, the less he wanted to stay.

"It's not as deep as it looks," Dana reassured. "I think it will heal alright."

"Thanks," said Matt.

"I can't waste any more time here," said Balder, impatiently. The limp body of Targon was draped over his shoulder and weighed him down. "We're asking for trouble by hanging about."

"Balder, take this boy along, too. Dorin will know what to do," Norak suggested.

"Are you crazy? We'll be taking a huge risk," Balder replied. "Hiding Targon is bad enough without taking on a stranger too."

"Yes, but we can't leave him here," Norak said. "You'll be virtually handing the boy a death sentence."

Matt found the strength to utter, "Please don't leave me here."

"Well, Balder?" Dana begged.

"Okay, okay," said Balder reluctantly. "I don't have time to argue about this, but I think it's a mistake. Come on boy, get to your feet. I guess you're coming with me." He shifted the position of Targon on his shoulder and moved closer to the doorway.

Matt was suddenly hopeful. He was no longer alone, and for a fleeting moment he felt safer.

"Thanks, Balder," said Dana. Matt saw a faint smile curl from her thin lips.

"Okay, okay," said Balder again. "Now you two get going before we have a dozen Protectors looking for us!"

Matt watched Dana and Norak head down the corridor

towards the huge swing doors. Balder set off in the opposite direction and staggered along to the first corner. He peered slowly round, motioning to Matt to stay back against the wall. They rounded the corner and continued to creep along in the dim light.

Voices could be heard approaching from a corridor on the left. Balder turned quickly. Matt could see fear written across his face.

"Protectors!" he said, shoving Matt backward into a small room that they had passed moments before.

He lifted Targon off his shoulders and lay the boy on the floor out of sight from the doorway. Balder crouched with his back against the wall and placed his hand gently over Targon's mouth. Matt's heart began to race. Having just escaped the Protectors, he was not quite ready to face them again.

He looked at the man who was helping him to safety. Perspiration was running down his face from a thick crop of jet-black hair. He had a bushy mustache to match, which ended in fine points close to his chin.

The voices grew louder, passed by and then faded slowly. Matt drew in breath. His heart slowed again. Balder rose, and heaved Targon onto his other shoulder.

"Let's go," he snapped.

They continued to a small flight of stairs on the right. Matt was tired. He lagged behind.

"Keep up!" Balder panted, struggling to climb the steps with the weight of Targon on his back. The arms, which encircled the boy, were strong. Matt guessed by his physique that Balder was a young man, but the lines on his face made him appear as old as Matt's father.

At the top, a bright circular room appeared slightly more inviting. Many doors faced them. Each had a small window at the side. Tables and chairs, grouped in sixes, filled the whole of the common area. Another enormous glass dome covered the entire room and a large three-sided movie screen was suspended from the central roof supports. The blue sky invitingly hovered overhead. Matt stretched out his arm almost willing himself to be beyond the inhospitable environment and out in the late afternoon sunshine.

"We should be safe for a while. Protectors rarely visit the Sleeping Rooms," Balder told Matt, as he tottered across to the far side of the circle.

Balder knocked gently on one of the small glass panes. An elderly bearded man, clothed in a long white robe, appeared at the door and beckoned them inside.

"Targon's bad, real bad," said Balder, laying the boy down on Dorin's bed. Dorin gazed at Matt and raised his eyebrows, but said nothing, deciding that Targon needed his attention first.

Matt stared at the lifeless figure. Targon was a boy, much the same age as he; his blonde hair was long and wet with perspiration. Apart from the strange baggy blue pants and tight tunic top, he could have been one of Matt's classmates.

Dorin knelt on the floor and opened Targon's eyelids, gazing at the boy's pupils. "Get me some water. The boy has a high fever, but I think he'll survive."

Balder opened a cupboard and selected a cloth which

he then soaked with water in a tiny washbasin at the far end of the room. He handed the wet toweling square to Dorin, who lovingly patted it across Targon's forehead. A second cloth was handed to Matt. The bleeding had just about stopped, but his hand was covered in dried blood, and the wound was painful to touch.

Matt licked his lips; they were so dry. He looked longingly at the basin full of water. Balder caught his expression and handed him a small glass which was guzzled in seconds.

Dorin shakily got to his feet. He looked at Matt's hand and undid the sheet from the end of the mattress. A long strip of linen was ripped off and the rough edge of the sheet hastily tucked back underneath and out of sight. Dorin bound Matt's hand tightly. He eyed Matt with suspicion but still asked no questions. It was as if he knew that Matt meant even more trouble, and for now, Targon was enough for him to deal with. "We'll have to keep Targon hidden for a few days," Dorin said.

"Then what will we do with him? Protector 13 thinks he has been disposed of, so the records will show that he is no longer in existence. We can hardly take him back to the work room and we can't keep him hidden forever," said Balder.

"I have been told that there are ways. I shall make inquiries quietly tomorrow. The boy won't be well enough for several days yet," replied Dorin. "That will give me enough time to make plans. In the meantime we must take turns watching him."

"You must find the Liberators," Matt spoke up, feeling

slightly refreshed.

Balder and Dorin swung round and stared at Matt.

"You'd better tell me who he is!" Dorin finally said.

"Don't know. I haven't had a chance to ask with all the worry over Targon," explained Balder. "We found him wandering around downstairs. He asked Dana for help. He was hurt and seemed scared, so I brought him with me. I didn't know what else to do."

Dorin sat down on the floor next to Targon and placed his head in his hands. "Zang it!" he exclaimed. "Another runaway! This gets worse! Now you want me to find a way out for *two* boys? What were you thinking of, Balder?"

"Well we couldn't just leave him for the Protectors to find!" Balder snapped.

"I may be able to help you to freedom. I just don't know my way around Zaul," Matt stuttered.

"You, help?" Dorin laughed. "You don't even look like one of us!"

"I'm not one of you. My name is Matt. I'm from the year 2010, and you're in my computer game!"

"I beg your pardon?" Balder said.

"You're in my computer game," said Matt again, pulling out his black laptop from inside his denim jacket. "This is the year 2540, correct? If I can work out how to beat the Protectors and destroy the Keeper of the Kingdom, I can save you all!"

"The boy's ill," said Dorin.

Matt studied their expressions and realized how silly he sounded to them.

"I think you'd better leave right now," said Balder.

"We've got more important things to worry about with Targon here, than listening to your gibberish."

"No, wait, please," begged Matt, wondering how he could begin to convince them. "How did I know about the Liberators? I'm right, aren't I?"

"Never heard of them!" said Balder, getting quite angry. Dorin was quiet for a moment. He walked up to Matt and looked deep into his eyes.

"I have," he said quietly. "Go on then, I'm listening. You've got my attention Matt, or whatever your name is."

Balder gave Dorin a quizzical look and threw his hands up in the air in disbelief.

Matt stared back into the old man's trusting face.

"Thank you," he said softly. "See this black box? Well, this is a small personal computer, similar to the ones attached to some of the walls around here that I've seen the Protectors use."

"Computers, eh?" Dorin questioned. "They are called 'Magic boxes'. The Commanders and Protectors can open doors, speak to strange images and magic themselves away by touching one."

"They're not magic, really. Look, I'll show you," said Matt opening the lid.

Dorin hastily backed away. Balder shielded his face, terrified of the small black object.

"We cannot look at a magic box. It will harm us," said Balder.

"It won't. Please trust me. Look, I am just like you," said Matt, pinching his flesh and raising his wounded hand in the air. "I'm not a Protector, but I can use this without injury."

"But you say you're not one of us either," said Balder. "So, how do we know it won't hurt us?"

"I'm still human, even if I am from a different time."

Matt turned on the power. *Please work*, he prayed. The green light appeared. Relieved, he continued and watched the Windows 2010 logo appear on the screen. Dorin and Balder were not ready for the sudden appearance of the bright light and found themselves looking at a multitude of color. Matt hoped that the battery was not dead. It had now been several hours since it was last charged up, but his new power pack was supposed to give him 15 hours of playing time.

"See, it won't hurt you."

Matt clicked on the icon for his new game, and watched the words "***Keeper of the Kingdom***" scroll across the screen. Dorin and Balder leaned forward transfixed. Balder stretched out his finger and slowly touched the screen, tracing the words and gasping in delight.

"How do you make this magic?" Dorin asked.

"It isn't magic, it is just a machine which we can control. Your Commanders and Protectors obviously have this technology, too. You Workers have just not been allowed education or access to it. You operate machines - I heard the noise downstairs as you wheeled Targon out on the trolley."

"Yes, but they are nothing like this." Balder said.

"Maybe not, but machines nevertheless, controlled by man. It is just that these machines, called computers, are more advanced than you have seen before or understand."

Dorin nodded thoughtfully. "The boy speaks sense. So tell us how your computer can help, and what you know of the Liberators."

"Well, this morning I installed my new game, **Keeper of the Kingdom,** and read the instructions. Briefly, the game takes place on Earth in the year 2540 when the planet is divided into thousands of small fighting Kingdoms. The idea of the game is to rescue the Workers of the 'Kingdom of Zaul' and set them free from the Protectors by using the Liberators. But, to win, I have to destroy the Keeper of the Kingdom, too. As it is a new game, I hadn't got very far with the exact details."

"So, how does this all effect us?" Dorin asked, completely losing Matt's line of thinking.

"Is this not Zaul? Am I not in the year 2540?"

Dorin and Balder nodded. "True," they said.

"You are in my game, honestly. I don't know how I came to be here, but I am, and I can't say I really like it. It is one thing playing the game on a screen and controlling all the moves every character makes, but it's another to be in the game and not have any control over events."

"Well, I'm sorry, but you must understand, this is all very hard for us to accept. You really expect us to believe that we are some kind of figures in a child's game?" Dorin laughed.

"I know, it all sounds unbelievable, even to me as I stand here telling you this. But I can tell you anything you want to know about the Protectors, you - the Workers, and the Keeper. Unfortunately I hadn't quite got to the part where I had to find the Liberators." Matt scratched his head. This worried him. *Somehow I have to find the game instructions,* he thought. *Why didn't I install them when I loaded the game?*

"If you know so much about us and are really 'playing a game,' tell us what we Workers do and why," said Dorin, convinced that Matt would be unable to answer.

"You operate machines that manufacture Xeleron. This is a chemical, which the Protectors use in their weapons. Your people are currently at war with the 'Kingdom of Prall' and so you work twelve hours a day to keep up with the demand for Xeleron needed to win the battles. The chemical is deadly to the touch, and breathing in the fumes given off as it is manufactured makes people very ill, and often kills."

The room fell quiet. Dorin and Balder looked stunned. They sat in silence on the floor staring at this knowledgeable boy holding the colored screen.

"There, how was that?" Matt asked.

"Zang it!" Balder declared.

Dorin still seemed a little skeptical. "So, you seem to know an awful lot. Perhaps you have just been snooping down our corridors for longer than we think? I'm sure that you could have learned a lot by listening to the Protectors. Perhaps you are a spy sent by the Keeper to find the Liberators?"

"Everyone keeps talking about Liberators. I wish you'd tell me who the 'zang' they are!" Balder said angrily.

"The Liberators are a group of people who know a way to freedom and want to overthrow the Keeper and the Protectors," explained Matt. "They are growing in number daily and manage to get many Workers out of here and onto the surface of the planet. There are now so many Liberators that they are becoming a real threat to the Keeper. Whether or not you know it, the war that your Kingdom is fighting is futile."

"And just why is that?" Dorin asked. "Our daily existence depends upon the Xeleron that we manufacture for the war."

"Your neighbors, the Pralls, want peace, but the Keeper is determined to gain more territory at the expense of millions of lives. The human Commanders are greedy men enjoying power, and the Cybergons are programmed to fight and serve without question. They have no knowledge that the Pralls want peace. I'm sure that if they could be reprogrammed, they might join any rebellion against the Keeper."

"That doesn't seem a possibility to me. There are too many–several hundred Cybergon Protectors who guard us to begin with, not to mention the thousands of Cybergon Soldiers that are fighting the war," Dorin added.

"I agree, but for now I think that the important thing is to somehow make contact with the Liberators," Matt said.

"You mean you don't know how?" Balder asked. "Look, I have to get back to my work post or Protector 13 will not accept my excuse. I have no more time for this utter rubbish. I'll leave you to decide what to do with him, Dorin. I'll see you later." Balder shrugged his shoulders and shook his head in annoyance as he left. The door slammed shut behind him.

"I thought you said you could help us?" Dorin said,

disappointed. "Although I'm not about to believe that we are a part of your so-called, 'computer game', I *was* beginning to believe that with your incredible knowledge of our situation, you might really be of help." Dorin looked depressed.

"I really think I can, but it will take time and somehow I have to find the game information. I dropped the CD-ROM on the upper level when Protector 21 and Protector 34 were chasing me, probably before I climbed the metal pillar. I have to locate it before they do. Will you help me?"

"I have no choice but to help you. Our lives are miserable. We live in constant fear of immediate elimination and many of the weak and elderly die each day from Xeleron fumes," said Dorin. "The people of Zaul simply can't continue like this. The Liberators are our only hope, regardless of any game that you say we are in or not in."

"When I retrieve the CD-ROM..." Matt began.

"I think that you mean 'if,'" said Dorin, interrupting.

"Then, I'll have to be very careful searching for and using the information on my computer," continued Matt, ignoring Dorin's pessimism. "I don't want to make any mistakes because somehow, I'm now in the game with you!"

"Oh, great, so you're saying that even if you retrieve your CD-ROM thing, by making a wrong move in this game, you could obliterate us all?" Dorin asked.

Matt didn't reply. The thought was too scary.

Chapter 3

Dana and Norak had positioned themselves back at their work posts. Dana retied her long brown hair and then wound it up tightly in her worker's cap. It was necessary to keep all hair away from the chemicals, so Workers were given the option of wearing the standard hat or having their hair cut short. The smell in the laboratory was vile, and even though their faces were covered with masks, breathing was not easy. Dana's hands brushed her cheeks as she tied the gauze mask tightly behind her head. It saddened her that she had not yet turned twenty years old and already her skin was rough and lined.

Several Protectors stood on metal platforms at various points around the huge room, surveying the progress. Each was dressed in the same navy blue uniform, armed, prepared for trouble and quite willing to kill to keep order. Dana knew that attempting to escape or refusing to work would have serious consequences. Those workers who rebelled were spared no mercy and eliminated immediately. In the Kingdom of Zaul there were no small crimes, no minor punishments, no prisons for petty offenders. From age ten, you worked and obeyed the law or died. Dana wondered how many other similar laboratories existed. She knew of three others but assumed there were many more, each probably holding up to two hundred workers. She sighed. Her surroundings were dismal and she spent almost half of her life in this one room. Unlike the domed Sleeping Rooms where at least she could see the sun and the wonderful blue sky, the laboratory was lit artificially. The white walls, broken only by the Protector's metal platforms, merged with the ceiling. The environment was claustrophobic at times.

Protector 13 came up behind Dana and placed his hand on her shoulder. She shuddered with fear as his grip tightened.

"Worker Dana," he said. "Did you dispose of Targon properly?"

"Yes, Protector. Here is his ID tag, Protector, Sir."

Protector 13 reached out and yanked the gold tag from Dana's grasp. He nodded in satisfaction.

"I can see Worker Norak but not Worker Balder."

"Worker Balder had to visit the Cleanliness room, Protector," Dana lied convincingly. Workers were allowed frequent short bathroom visits, but it was usual to ask permission first.

"He seems to be taking a long time." Protector 13 glanced at the bronze 'Command Ring' located on the middle finger of his left hand. "He has been gone over fifteen minutes now."

"I'm sure Balder will return shortly, Protector. He was feeling a little unwell." Dana covered for him.

Protector 13 tapped the 'Command Ring' twice and

placed his finger up to his mouth.

"Protector 157, please find Worker Balder in Green Sector. He should be visiting the Cleanliness Room."

At that moment the doors opened and a flustered Balder entered and returned to his workstation. Dana smiled at him with relief. Protector 13 nodded in approval and canceled the order given to Protector 157.

"A long Cleanliness visit, Balder," he said, walking up to him.

"Yes, I'm sorry Protector. My next one will be shorter." Balder reassured him.

"So be it," he said, "I shall be watching you carefully. Return to work."

Protector 13 eyed him with slight suspicion and then returned to his platform. Balder twirled the ends of his mustache between his fingers and then winked at Norak and Dana, indicating that he had successfully completed his mission.

Dana returned to her work. The fluorescent tube above her small laboratory bench flickered and hurt her eyes, but she would not be granted a new one until it died. She picked up the test tube containing the chemicals she had been mixing earlier and studied the solution. The color did not look right. She would have to measure the contents again. Targon's faked death had distracted her, and she would be punished if the Xeleron mixture were not accurate. Too much or too little of one of the vital ingredients could change the whole chemical balance.

The large metal doors were suddenly thrust open, and Commander Z stormed into the room, closely followed by

21. The five Protectors stood at attention, weapons loaded and aimed at the Workers below. Dana stopped what she was doing and glanced in Balder's direction. Panic swept over her. Had Targon been discovered?

"Welcome, Commander," said Protector 13.

"Let us dispense with the formality, 13," the Commander replied.

"Yes, Sir!" 13 stood to attention. "How can we be of assistance to the Commander?"

Commander Z climbed the steps of the central platform and faced the Workers. He removed his black leather gloves and hurriedly undid the top two buttons of his jacket. He began to flick the gloves angrily against the metal handrail of the platform. Dana felt uncomfortable. The Commander's mood was not a good sign. This was no ordinary inspection visit.

"Roll call!" He shouted. "Protector 21."

"Yes, Commander."

As they had performed numerous times previously, the workers left their positions and filed into five lines at the front of the laboratory. Dana took her place on the front row in between Balder and Norak. Balder stood steady, unflinching, seemingly unconcerned. Norak grabbed Dana's hand briefly and tightly squeezed it as if to reassure her that everything was fine. She looked up into his rugged face to see a warm encouraging smile and then looked ahead at the frightening frame of Commander Z. His eyes penetrated the lines of Workers through the slit in his hood.

"Proceed with Line 1, " the Commander ordered 21.

"Annder, Leoni, Calvert, Sergin. . ." Protector 21

bellowed across the room. As each name was called from the list, the Worker stepped forward and raised a hand.

"Balder, Dana, Norak, Targon. . ." Protector 21 continued. He hesitated when there was no response to the name Targon and turned to face Commander Z.

"Targon died earlier today and was disposed of accordingly," Protector 13 announced.

Commander Z leaned over and whispered something to 21. Dana's heart was racing. She was now very worried.

"At what time was Targon disposed of?" Protector 21 questioned.

"Not more than one hour ago," answered 13.

Commander Z seemed annoyed at this response and whispered yet again to 21.

"Who disposed of Targon?" Protector 21 asked.

Dana, Balder and Norak slowly stepped forward. Even Balder was now concerned. He felt his hands trembling and tried to stay calm. He wondered if the boy Matt had betrayed them after all.

"How long ago would you say you disposed of the body?" Commander Z asked Norak.

"It is as Protector 13 says Commander, Sir, less than an hour ago," Norak replied.

"Are you sure that it could not have been two to three hours ago?" Commander Z continued with the questioning.

"Positive, Commander."

"And Targon was without a doubt dead?"

"Yes, Commander, Protector 13 checked the body before we left for the Disposal Room."

"Thank you, Norak. You may step back." The

Commander waved his hand indicating that for now he was finished with him.

Norak sighed with relief. He felt that he had done well and answered the Commander convincingly.

"Worker Dana, do you know the approximate age of Targon?"

"No, Commander Sir, but I did give his ID tag to Protector 13 when I returned from the Disposal Room," Dana said.

"Yes, of course, the ID tag. Thank you, Worker Dana. Protector 13, let me see it immediately."

13 produced the item and handed it to Commander Z, who took his time fingering the gold disc and studying the engraving.

"Young to die, was he not?" Commander Z asked 13.

"Not really, Sir. He was a sickly boy and the fumes in this laboratory often claim the lives of the less sturdy youngsters."

"So be it. Continue with the roll call, Protector 21."

Dana drew in breath and stepped backwards. Something was definitely wrong, but what, she was not sure. She had a feeling that perhaps it was the boy Matt they were looking for and not Targon. She glanced at Balder who by now had come to the same conclusion.

The roll call finished, and the Workers were dismissed back to work. Balder watched Commander Z and Protector 21 whisper in the corner. The Commander was unquestionably agitated. He pulled on his gloves roughly and stormed down the main aisle towards the double doors.

"We must locate the intruder before we see the Keeper," he snapped at Protector 21 as he passed by Balder.

The horn sounded indicating the end of the shift. It had been a long twelve hours. Dana quickly removed her mask and caught up with Balder and Norak as they left the laboratory for the Sleeping Rooms. They climbed the stairs in silence and headed directly for Dorin's room, checking to make sure that the Commander was not having them followed.

"Take over while I'm working. Targon is still not out of danger. He needs plenty of liquids, and you must keep him cool until the fever breaks," Dorin instructed while putting on his coveralls.

"And the boy, Matt?" Balder questioned.

"He can be trusted. I'm not totally convinced by all of his arguments, but a lot of what he says makes sense so we cannot afford to ignore his information. The boy may be our ticket to freedom. For now, we listen to what he suggests and help him in any way we can. He needs to find a lost part to his computer, a C something wasn't it?" Dorin asked, turning to Matt sitting quietly on the floor in the corner of the room.

"CD-ROM," Matt confirmed, getting to his feet.

"And where is this likely to be located?" Norak asked.

"I lost it earlier when Protector 21 and Commander Z spotted me," said Matt.

"So, that explains the Commander's sudden appearance and 'Roll Call' earlier," said Dana, very relieved that the visit had been in no way connected with Targon.

"So, they're still looking for me?" Matt asked.

"But of course, and they won't give up either. Describe exactly where you were," said Balder.

"The long hall had many huge angular metal pillars which supported a glass domed roof rather like the one here above the Sleeping Rooms. There were no windows and only one door. I took a steep spiral staircase to escape, which brought me down to just outside the laboratory where I met you."

"Zang it!" exclaimed Balder. "The boy is talking about the Forbidden Hall! No wonder you've caused such a rumpus! You obviously did not realize that only Protectors and Commanders are allowed on that level?"

"Believe me, it wasn't by choice. I somehow landed there and, come to think of it, I was about to enter the Forbidden Hall in my game when my computer locked up."

"Any Worker who is caught on that level, or even climbing the stairs to that level, is automatically terminated," Norak said.

"It is very heavily patrolled by Protectors. There have been many who have tried to find a way out, and have not returned alive," Balder added.

"Almost twelve hours every day working in the laboratory is enough to make any Worker decide that it is worth taking the risk. The stairs are right by the laboratory doors and are an inviting prospect to the weak or sick as they leave after a shift," said Dana.

A shrill siren sounded. Dorin rapidly tied his shoulder length white hair into a small ponytail behind his head.

"That's the signal for the start of my shift," he said for Matt's benefit. "I'll be late if I don't go now. We don't want any attention drawn to this room. Dana, I suggest you all take turns sleeping and getting food. Try to get extra for the boys."

"Don't worry, Dorin. All of our lives are on the line here. We'll be careful," Dana reassured him.

"Oh, and see if you can find a way to locate Matt's 'C' thing," Dorin added as he left.

"CD-ROM," Matt corrected.

Targon was looking better. Color had returned to his cheeks, and he was sleeping more easily. Matt played with the food in front of him. Nothing on his plate looked particularly appetizing. The long green things tasted very bitter and did not resemble any kind of vegetable known to him. What he assumed to be meat tasted like rubber, and his drink slipped down his throat in a slimy sort of way. Matt watched as Norak and Balder hungrily demolished everything on their plates.

"The Kitchen Workers prepare good food, do they not?" Balder said.

"Yes, very good, but I'm afraid I'm not hungry at the moment," Matt politely replied.

"Do you mind if Norak and I share what you don't want?" Balder asked, showing some embarrassment.

"No, that's fine," said Matt. He happily pushed his plate across the small metal table in Balder's direction.

"We only get two meals a day, one before our shift and one after. Although it is good, there is never really enough," Norak explained.

"How do you grow your food underground without light?" Matt asked.

"We don't," said Norak.

"But I thought that Workers were not allowed on the surface?"

"So, you don't know everything about us from your computer game then?" Balder teased. He wouldn't have admitted it, but he was beginning to like the boy, Matt.

"As I said, I had only been playing a few hours when my computer locked up on me. I'm sure I would have found out if I had been able to play a little longer!"

"Apart from Workers and Protectors, we also have gardeners whose specific job it is to provide enough food for the Kingdom. They are escorted to the surface daily and guarded by the Protectors while they work," said Norak.

"We are told that the gardens are very beautiful. We also have huge greenhouses, with glass roofs similar to the one above our Sleeping Rooms. It is a privilege to be a gardener. Most Zauls are born gardeners but a good Worker can also earn the right to become one after ten years below ground," added Balder.

"Wow, it sounds preferable to working in the laboratory or kitchen," said Matt.

"That it is. I would give anything for one day up there in the sun," Balder sighed.

Dana entered and walked over to the bed where Targon was still sleeping. She placed the back of her hand on his forehead.

"He's much better I think. Norak, your turn to get a few hours sleep."

"Sure, I'm ready for it. See you later," he said, carrying out his dirty plate.

Dana sat down next to Matt at the small table in the corner of Dorin's room.

"How are you doing?" she asked, picking up his bandaged hand gently.

"Much better, thanks to you," said Matt, blushing. "I don't know what I would have done. I was so exhausted. Thanks for trusting and helping me."

"Think nothing of it," Dana smiled. "Anyway, from what I hear, you may be able to help us in return. So, have you had any thoughts about how we retrieve your C thing?"

"CD-ROM," Matt corrected for the third time. "No, I haven't yet."

"Well, I think it is time that we formulated some kind of plan. We can't keep you boys hidden here forever, and Dorin will be disappointed if we haven't at least discussed it by the time he returns," said Dana.

"Tell me about the various ways to access the Forbidden Hall," said Matt.

"Only two that I know of," Balder interjected.

Matt scratched his head. "The stairs, and through the concealed doors used by the Protectors, right?"

"Correct," said Balder.

"So, where does that leave us?" asked Dana.

"It means that he has to take a risk of not being seen on the stairs or find a way to use the Protector's Magic Box," Balder sighed.

"Computer, not Magic Box," Matt corrected again.

Balder smiled at the new vocabulary. "Computer," he

repeated.

"Do you think you could figure out our system?" Dana asked.

Matt didn't reply. He was deep in thought staring at the pipes on the ceiling and thinking back to his time in the Forbidden Hall. He visualized the long empty corridor, the steel pillars, the red tiled floor, the floor ducts. . .

Dana studied the expression on Matt's face. Her eyes lit up. "Have you thought of something?"

"Could be," he responded, still deep in thought.

"What? Tell us," said Balder impatiently.

"There were grids in the floor of the Forbidden Hall, all the way down the length of it. I remember thinking how strange they were because of their large size, and also because I could see light through them. Are they some kind of heating or air system?"

Dana shook her head. "Not that I know of. Our air, hot and cold, comes through circular vents overhead, like those," she said pointing to one on the ceiling. "I have no idea what you are speaking of."

"I think I do," said Balder, "but of course I have never actually seen them to be sure."

"So, what do you think they are?" asked Matt and Dana in unison.

"Dana, where does the Xeleron go when it leaves our laboratory?"

"It is placed in the insulated elevator and sent upwards."

"Right, and do you remember what is at the top of the elevator shaft on the ceiling?" Balder asked her excitedly.

"Yes, you're right—it's a large white grid! You don't think

that the conveyor system for the Xeleron runs under the floor of the Forbidden Hall do you?" she asked.

"That's my reasoning, yes. It has to be transported over to the weapons store somehow, doesn't it?" Balder was getting quite excited.

"And the weapons store is past our Sleeping Rooms on the upper level - another place we are not allowed," said Dana, beginning to follow what Balder was thinking.

"So, it sounds highly probable that the Xeleron is sent by that route," said Matt with a huge grin across his face. "Do you think that the conveyor shaft is wide enough for me to crawl along?"

"Without a doubt, judging by the width of the crates containing Xeleron that we send up," said Balder. "Each crate has large wheels on the base, so I would imagine that there is some kind of track on which they move along. You may have to crawl along a rail of some kind."

"As long as it is wide enough, I'll find a way," Matt said.

"Xeleron has to be kept in the light or it becomes inoperative," said Dana. "Therefore the conveyor shafts would have to be brightly lit. If you saw light from through these grids it only strengthens Balder's theory." Dana grinned broadly.

"Presumably Xeleron is an explosive material?" asked Matt.

"Correct," said Balder.

"How often will Xeleron move along the shaft? Because I wouldn't want to be in there when a load is being transported!" Matt grimaced at the thought.

"The elevators are only operated at the end of each shift

unless a higher quantity is needed on any day," said Balder. "So, if we can find a way to get you into the elevator shaft, you could probably climb up and follow the conveyor system under the floor."

"And how would I get out through a grid, assuming that I can see where my CD-ROM has fallen?" Matt asked.

"Good question. Dana and I will try and get a look at how it is attached. I can't honestly say that I have ever had the need to look at one closely before."

"Well, if we can find a way, this seems by far the safest method to get you up there without being seen," said Dana excitedly. "I don't think I've had this much fun in years!"

"The sooner we do it, the better. A shiny silver disc lying in an empty hall will be spotted easily," said Matt, "and I really need to load it, to find out how to contact the Liberators and how to destroy the Keeper."

"Tomorrow then. It has to be tomorrow. I'm sure Dorin will have some good ideas when he gets back," said Balder.

"For now Matt, from Earth 2010, you'd better get some sleep. In fact, so had you, Balder," said Dana.

Chapter 4

Dorin returned from his work shift and placed the small metal key into Matt's palm. The end was cylindrical and hollow, unlike any key he had seen before.

"This will open the white grids."

"How did you get it?" Matt asked.

"I took a great risk acquiring it from a Worker in the Maintenance Shop, so don't lose it. I won't be able to get another."

Matt pushed the key deep into his front jean pocket for safety. He turned his attention to a rough map that Dorin had scratched with a fork on the inside of his cupboard door.

"Now remember, once we get you inside the elevator shaft, you will have no more than ten hours to make your search and return. Hopefully, you won't need anywhere near that length of time."

"So, you think that the shaft will pass by the top of the spiral staircase and then the Protector's Rooms?" asked Matt, studying the diagram.

"Yes. I'm pretty certain that the two are quite close together, so be very careful."

"How do I get out of the elevator shaft once I'm done?"

"Balder, Norak and Dana will get you in at the beginning of their shift, and you must be back two hours before the end of their shift, when the Workers start to load the Xeleron into the elevator. Dana loads the crates as part of her job. She will be there to get you out, so don't worry. They have a good plan. Just concentrate on being back on time."

Matt nodded. "I'm ready then."

"They'll be here any minute as there are only fifteen minutes between shift change, so any last questions?" Dorin asked.

"Don't think so. Thanks for your help, Dorin."

"You're welcome, boy. I'm counting on you as my ticket to freedom, so don't let me down and get caught!"

Balder led Matt back down the stairs from the Sleeping Rooms. He paused at the foot and quickly glanced each way down the corridor.

"All clear," he announced.

They walked speedily towards the laboratory doors. Balder pushed one slightly ajar and peered round.

"Okay, quick," he said, and shoved Matt in before him.

Dana and Norak were waiting impatiently by a white walled area that protruded into the room by several feet. Matt paused to look around the laboratory. Like everywhere else that he had seen so far, there were whitewashed walls and no outside windows. Metal platforms, about ten feet high, were attached periodically around the room. They were surrounded by guardrails, accessible only via a vertical ladder with narrow rungs, and bolted firmly to the wall. Rows of small circular aluminum tables, each with an attached stool and several molded trays containing chemicals, were covered with racks of test tubes and machines that resembled enormous mixers and liquidizers.

"Come on Matt, hurry it up!" Dana whispered. "We have less than five minutes before the Protectors enter for the next shift. If we are caught in here when they arrive we're dead!" She pressed a green glass button, and two shiny metallic doors opened.

"This is it. Good luck Matt," she said, pushing him inside the shaft.

"Don't forget, you have ten hours and no more," reminded Norak.

Matt nodded and started to climb using the mechanism which lifted the crates of Xeleron for a foothold. Dana watched him disappear from view and then hurriedly closed the doors.

"Right, let's get out of here fast!" said Balder, frantically.

They raced through the swing doors just as the Protector's concealed entrance in the ceiling started to vibrate. Dana, Balder and Norak paused in the corridor to get their breath.

"That was too close for me," said Dana.

"I thought you were enjoying the excitement?" Balder teased.

"I was, when I didn't think it was me taking the risks!" Dana laughed.

The shrill siren sounded.

"Right, to work then. Are you ready for this?" Norak

asked, walking back towards the laboratory doors.

"Well, it's too late to pull out now. We got Matt into the Conveyor system, so we will have to get him out again," Balder said.

"I know, but the next ten hours are going to pass very slowly," said Dana. "I do hope he finds his C thing."

"CD-ROM," Balder proudly corrected with a smile.

It was hot and bright inside the shaft, but plenty wide enough for Matt to crawl along. The conveyor system consisted of two metal rails similar in appearance to a train track, so it was easy for Matt to move in between them. He strained to see through the first white grid. By pressing his face to the mesh, he was able to catch a glimpse of the corner of the computer terminal used by 34 the day before. He tried to remember where he had run before he had climbed the pillar, but his mind was a blank. Matt knew that he would have to open the grid to see the floor properly.

The little key was difficult to manipulate in the holes, particularly when his hand was still quite painful. Matt struggled with each corner and finally loosened four tiny white pegs. The grid shifted. Matt's heart raced. He listened for any sounds of movement before moving the grid to one side and pushing his head up through the hole.

His position in the hall was exactly as he had guessed. Scanning the floor in every direction was easy. There were no furniture, drapes or other obstacles to obscure something the size of a CD-ROM. Disappointed, he decided to move on to the next grid which he knew to be level with the spiral staircase. Perhaps he had dropped the disc near the base of the pillar?

Matt replaced the cover, tightly screwed up the four corner pegs and tucked the key back in his pocket. He crawled another fifty yards before reaching the second grid. Looking up he could make out the handrail of the staircase to his left, and so set about undoing the corner pegs. This time the grid would not shift an inch.

"Zang it!" Matt copied Balder's expression with frustration. He raised his clenched fist and firmly struck the corner in an attempt to set it free. He gritted his teeth in pain as his cut hand came into contact with the grid edge. He was about to hit the second corner with his other hand when the sound of heavy boots stopped him. Matt lay motionless, his heart pumping away furiously as the feet came closer and then paused directly above the grid. He could see the black heel of one of the Protector's boots standing on the edge.

"Did you hear something, Protector 305?"

"I do not know, Protector 96."

"We must be sure. Was it not here that the intruder was seen?"

"You are correct, 305. Commander Z has instructed intensified patrols in this area."

"Let us be certain; I would not like to experience the wrath of the Commander if we allow the intruder to escape during our patrol."

"Agreed. Let us walk the corridor one more time," said Protector 96.

"Arm your Xeleray," said Protector 305.

Matt trembled as he heard the familiar "clunk-click" of the weapon being loaded. The boots became faint as the

Protectors walked the remaining length of the Forbidden Hall. Matt hurriedly pushed on the frame of the grid with both hands and felt it shift slightly under the force. He decided that he would have time to take a quick look across the floor before the guards returned.

The edge squeaked as he lifted one side just enough for his eyes to peer through. He started as far to the left as he could see and slowly studied every inch of floor between the large pillars and the far wall.

"Nothing," he mumbled miserably, "Where could it be?"

Bitterly disappointed, Matt lowered the grid back into position, pushed the pegs into place and lay perfectly still, waiting for the two Protectors to return. He heard the heavy boots faintly at first, then getting louder and finally passing by without incident.

Matt looked at his watch. Less than two hours had passed, so plenty of time remained. While he had the chance he must explore every possibility of retrieving the CD-ROM. The Conveyor shaft was perfectly straight, and looking ahead, it appeared to go on for miles. His knees were so sore from crawling and the cut in his hand was now bleeding again, but he knew that this would be his only chance.

The third grid, as Dorin had predicted looked up into the Protector's rooms. Matt pressed his face once again to the mesh and realized that he was sitting directly under a large metal table.

"It is a strange thing, is it not?"

"Indeed, Protector 21."

"Have you any idea what a shiny circular object in a

clear container might be used for?"

"Let me observe it more closely," said Protector 60.

Matt nearly banged his head on the grid with excitement as he realized his CD-ROM was being discussed. His excitement turned to despair. How could he possibly get it back from a room full of Protectors?

"It is indeed very peculiar. It appears to be like our BETAROMS but fifty times as big," said Protector 60.

"Some kind of prehistoric computer memory, you think?" Protector 21 laughed loudly. "It is said that Humans once had a great knowledge of the workings of computers before they let us take over and do everything for them."

"Look where trusting computers has got them!" Protector 60 joined in the laughter. "Now we are in virtual control and will soon have no need for the Human Commanders."

"Quiet, Protector 60. It is not yet time for the rebellion. You must keep these thoughts to yourself until we Cybergons are totally ready to take over."

Matt gasped in horror. Now he had no choice but to find a way to get the CD-ROM back immediately and help the Workers and Liberators. If he did not, the entire human race would face terrible slavery, under the Cybergons, until the end of time.

More boots entered the room.

"Protector's 305 and 96, is all well?" asked 21.

"We are not certain that all is well," said 96.

"That does not sound good. Commander Z will not be very happy with that answer. What causes you to be unsure?" asked 21, concerned.

"There was a puzzling noise in the Forbidden Hall, but we patrolled the length two times and could not see anything to make such a noise," said Protector 305.

Protector 21 got to his feet. "This is a most serious matter. We have not been able to locate the intruder. Perhaps he has somehow managed to evade our patrols? 60, come with us. We will make yet another search to be sure."

Suddenly the room was quiet. Matt realized that it was now or never. He fumbled in his pocket for the little key. His palms were sweaty with nerves as he hurriedly undid the first peg, then the second. The key dropped from his slippery hands as he started on the third.

"Zang it!" Matt wiped his wet palms on his jeans, felt for the key beneath his chest and continued. Finally the fourth peg fell out, and he shook the grid to free it. Matt sighed with relief as it moved easily to one side.

The CD-ROM lay on the table where 21 had put it down in his eagerness to catch the intruder. Matt grabbed it and hurriedly lowered himself back into the conveyor shaft, pulling the grid into place after him. He knew that he must replace the pegs so that the Protectors would not learn of this new and wonderful spy tunnel. It might be a very valuable route on future occasions for Workers or Liberators.

Matt looked at his watch again. It had now been five hours, well within the time limit, but he had a long way to crawl back and he was exceptionally tired. He paused in the shaft to rest, just out of sight of the Protector's room, and lay his head on his arms, shielding his eyes from the brightness of the tunnel.

The sound of boots overhead stirred Matt. He wiped his eyes, shook his head, and focused on the CD-ROM in his hands. The sudden realization that he had fallen asleep made him feel sick. Matt looked at his watch. Only forty minutes left before he had to be back. He had slept for several hours! A wave of panic swept over him—would he be able to make it back in the time?

He began to crawl as fast as he was able, but it was not easy with a computer disc in one hand. There had to be an easier way. Matt placed the case in his mouth and bit down gently on to the case. Now he had two free hands to support his body weight. How his legs ached and his injured hand throbbed, but the fear of meeting crate-loads of explosive Xeleron coming in the opposite direction spurred him on and numbed the pain. He concentrated intensely on every yard left to crawl, passing the grids in the Forbidden Hall, towards the shaft that led downwards into the laboratory.

Matt reached the end just as he heard the doors slide open. He climbed back down the elevator shaft, slipping slightly with exhaustion, to meet Dana's relieved and welcoming bright blue eyes.

"Thank goodness," she whispered, hauling him out and shoving him behind her. "Wait two minutes. Do not move until I say, and then walk quickly to the door."

Matt froze on the spot. It took every ounce of strength to remain standing. He listened to the peace in the room except for the quiet hum of machinery, wondering what Dana was waiting for.

"Ahhhhh!" screamed Balder, breaking the silence.

"What is it, Worker Balder?" asked Norak, playing along with the plan.

Protector 13 and two others climbed down from their platforms and raced over to where Balder was now lying on the floor clutching his hands.

"Worker Balder, do you need treatment?" Protector 13 asked without any emotion in his voice.

"Yes, I need some Antileron, quickly, the test-tube spilled on my hand," screamed Balder in genuine pain.

"Let me see," Protector 13 said, turning over Balder's hands. The skin was raw and peeling.

"So be it. Protector 157 and 214 leave your platforms and get the Antileron from the treatment rooms."

All five Protectors were now occupied, and the chatter of the Workers worrying about Balder created a wonderful diversion.

"Now! Go now," said Dana, pushing Matt away from her in the direction of the double doors.

Matt slowly walked towards the corridor, keeping low behind the workers. Once out of the laboratory, he raced along the corridor, around the corner and up the stairs to the safety of Dorin's room.

"Dorin, Dorin," he beat on the glass window, "let me in."

The elderly man greeted him with a hug.

"Did you get it?" he asked anxiously.

Beaming from ear to ear, Matt held up the shiny disc.

"Got it!" he announced and collapsed on the floor at Dorin's feet.

Chapter 5

Matt opened his eyes slowly; a blond head peered over him.

"Hello Matt, from Earth 2010," smiled Targon.

Matt stretched his arms, threw off the blanket and sat up. He had been lying on the floor in Dorin's room. Targon looked weak perched on the edge of the bed, but he was well enough to be interested in his new roommate.

"Hello Targon, from Earth 2540," retorted Matt. "I'm glad to see you're so much better; you were pretty ill for a while there."

"You've slept a long time. You must have been exhausted. I've been watching you closely for hours, hoping you'd wake up," said Targon. "Dorin has told me everything about you, and nothing this exciting has ever happened around here!"

"I don't know about exciting. Pretty frightening, if you ask me!"

"I've been looking at those brown dots over your nose and cheeks. Does everyone have speckled skin in your time?"

Matt laughed. "I think you must be referring to my

freckles."

"Freckles, what are those exactly?" Targon asked.

"They're pigments in the skin which appear darker when you've been in the sun. Where I come from tons of people have freckles."

"I'd give anything to be able to go out in the sun," said Targon, sadly. "Sometimes I just stand under the glass dome above the Sleeping Rooms and look at it shining in the sky. I can feel the tremendous warmth of its rays through the roof. Most days I don't get to see the sun at all because it's dark when I finish my work shift."

"How old are you?" Matt asked, changing the subject to something less depressing.

"Just turned thirteen."

"Same as me," Matt smiled.

Targon seemed surprised. "Really?"

Matt secretly thought how much younger Targon looked because of his smaller size. Yet his skin was already beginning to wrinkle. The effects of a poor diet, the chemicals in the laboratory and lack of fresh air and sunshine were clearly visible.

"Is Dana your mother?" Matt asked.

"No way! Dana's much too young." It was Targon's turn to laugh. "But I guess she looks a lot older. My mother is a gardener. I'm only allowed to see her once a week."

"Gee, that seems a bit tough."

"It's the way here. When we get to ten years old, we start the jobs assigned to us. My mother was a Worker too, but because of her good behavior, the Protectors offered her a job as a gardener. She didn't want to go, but I insisted. The chemicals in the laboratory were making her sick; she would have died if she had stayed. What work do you do?"

"In the year 2010, we have to go to school instead of work. After that we can choose what job we do."

"What is school?" Targon asked.

"It is where I learn about computers," said Matt putting it very simply so that Targon might understand. He picked up his laptop from the floor, and took the CD-ROM out of the protective case.

"Dorin told me about your computer thing," said Targon, straining to see as Matt opened the lid. "Will you show me how it works?"

Matt got up off the blanket and sat on the bed next to Targon. "Where's Dorin?"

"The siren went for shift change a few minutes ago, so he should be back anytime now."

The door opened as Targon spoke and Dorin walked in, stripping off his coveralls and undoing his hair.

"That feels better!" he groaned. "Ah! Matt boy, you are finally awake. We have all been anxious to see if this special CD-ROM thing works, after you went to so much trouble to get it back."

Not half as anxious as I! Matt thought, inserting the disc.

Dorin pulled up the chair alongside the bed and stared with fascination at the blank screen.

"Doesn't it work?" Dorin asked.

"It takes time for the computer to recognize the CD. Here we go." The Windows 2010 logo appeared again, and Targon gasped with delight.

"Now I must click '**Setup**' to start the installation of the disc," said Matt, showing Targon the words on the screen. "There, now we click '**Install Keeper of the Kingdom/Rules**' and then '**Enter**'".

Music suddenly filled the room. Images of the Kingdom of Zaul, its buildings and domes nestled amongst the wooded hills, flashed before Targon's eyes.

"Wow, that place is beautiful!" Targon commented.

"Don't you recognize it?" Matt asked.

"I believe it is Zaul," said Dorin sadly. "Is that what our glass domes look like from the outside?"

"Yes, it's a beautiful Kingdom that you live in."

"What a pity we can't see it for ourselves," said Targon with tears in his eyes.

"Maybe you will one day," Matt said, hopefully.

Suddenly the music changed to a loud march with drums and cymbals. Hundreds of Protectors strode across the screen realistically brandishing their Xelerays.

Targon squirmed uncomfortably. "Please stop, Matt, please," he begged, turning his head away.

"It's okay, Targon. The Protectors on the screen are just computer images."

Targon composed himself and continued to watch.

"Is that how many of them there are?" Dorin asked.

"There are many more than that I'm afraid," Matt replied.

The music stopped and a colorful screen showed a list of options.

"What does it say?" Targon asked.

Matt suddenly realized that Targon had never learned to read. He remembered that Dorin had drawn a plan without any writing on it and so assumed that he also could not read.

"It is called the '*Menu,*' and it is asking me to choose what I now want to do. As we need the Game Rules, I'll click on '*Rules*'. Now I must select what scenario instructions I need. As we want to find out about how to contact a Liberator, I must click on number 3, '*Liberators,*'" said Matt pointing to the third option on the list.

The screen changed again and video images of beautiful gardens and people planting seeds flashed in front of Targon.

"What is the picture telling us?" he asked.

"Be patient and listen to the voice; it should explain to us what to do," said Matt.

"You mean your computer speaks to us, too?" asked Targon.

"Sort of," said Matt, smiling to himself.

The music stopped, and the screen zoomed in on the workers in the gardens. A young woman stepped forward.

"Welcome, players of Keeper of the Kingdom. I am Thera, a Liberator. To find me and get my help, you must first enter the gardens of Zaul. I will pass by the kitchen entrance once every daylight hour. When you see me, hold up your thumb and forefinger on your right hand making the sign of an 'L'. I will return the sign. You must then do the same with your left hand turning the 'L' upside down and crossing it with the index finger of your right hand, so making an 'F' for freedom. Once this is done I will take you to meet Varl, the leader of the Liberators."

Thera faded from view and the list of options returned.

"Wow!" said Targon, totally in awe.

"Well, now we know what we have to do," said Matt, shutting down the computer to conserve the battery.

Dorin remained silent.

"You seem worried," said Matt.

"Yes, and rightly so; getting to the gardens will prove to be more difficult than retrieving your CD-ROM."

"But, I know we can do it!" said Targon excitedly.

"We? Not *you* my boy, you've got a long way to go before *you* are fully recovered," snapped Dorin. "The only place you're going in the next few days is the Cleanliness Room!"

Targon groaned and lay back on the bed.

"Maybe none of us have to go. If I can play the game and get myself to the gardens, then I would only have to click on the appropriate letters to meet Varl," said Matt.

"Well what are you waiting for? Try it!" said Dorin.

"There's a risk."

"It can't be greater than the risk you have just taken to get your CD-ROM?"

"I guess not. Okay, here goes."

Matt pulled up the Menu on the screen, Dorin impatiently leaning over his shoulder and breathing heavily on his neck. Matt clicked '*Single Player*,' '*Saved Game*' and '*Matt1*' and then waited for his saved game to come up. Nothing happened. The screen did not change. Matt followed the same routine again, hammering on the keys in frustration. Still nothing happened and the menu remained.

"What is it?" asked Dorin.

"I'm not sure," said Matt, attempting the same

commands for a third time.

"Is it broken?" Targon said, resuming his previous interest.

"No, it's not broken. Let me try a new game," said Matt, entering the commands to start fresh. Still the menu remained on the screen. Matt banged his hand on the keyboard angrily.   "Of course it won't load the game because it is already running, and I'm in it, attempting to control events from here. So, how can the computer load what is already being played?"

"That seems highly complicated," said Dorin.

"Well, I'm afraid it makes sense."

"So now what are our options?" Dorin asked.

"I guess we have to come up with yet another plan, this time to get me into the gardens," said Matt.

"Yeah, all right!" shouted Targon. "You see, I'll be well in no time. Then you'll have no reason to keep me from going."

"I suggest you conserve your energy and think about how we get Matt in," said Dorin.

"You bet," said Targon, lying back on the bed and staring up at the ceiling. "Leave it to Targon, there's a good brain between these ears!"

"While the genius here is thinking, I'm going to get food," chuckled Dorin. "My favorite kitchen worker is serving today and she always gives me plenty of extra. Hope you boys are hungry. Targon, you need to eat if you're going to get this brain working!"

Matt's stomach turned at the thought of what he might have to digest today, but he knew he must eat to stay alive.

"He can laugh at me, but I often come up with good ideas," said Targon.

"Well, I hope you come up with a good one today! You wanted to be able to stand in the sunshine one day soon. Your chance to do that may depend on your idea," said Matt.

"You think?"

"I know!" replied Matt. "Say, there isn't another conveyor system for taking food from the gardens to the kitchen, is there?"

"Sorry, you're out of luck. I heard about what you did to find your CD thing."

"Just a thought. How many corridors will we have to negotiate from here to the kitchens?"

"It's a long way, but they aren't patrolled very frequently by Protectors, so I don't see that being much of a problem," said Targon.

"So, what is the problem? Why is Dorin so concerned?" asked Matt, suddenly feeling confused.

"There are only two ways of getting to the gardens, through the kitchens and through the gardeners' sleeping rooms. Both entrances are heavily guarded. Zaul is never able to produce as much food as is needed by all the people, so the Commanders and Protectors are always concerned that any rebellion might start in that sector. There are at least twenty Protectors at any one time in the kitchens and even more in the Sleeping Rooms."

"Wow!" said Matt. "Sounds pretty grim."

"Believe me, it is not going to be easy. Until we find the Liberators we cannot trust anyone. The kitchen staff may turn you over to the Protectors, fearing for their own safety. Protectors have been known to kill ten Workers at a time for hiding a traitor."

"No wonder Dorin was so upset when Balder brought the two of us to his room."

"Dorin has helped Workers before, and so far no one has turned him in. Now you can see why they have to get me out of here!"

Matt sat in silence. This was not going to be easy. He had only been in Zaul for two days, but already he was missing home and the outdoors. He looked at Targon and wondered what a life underground with no hope of feeling the warmth of the sun must be like. It made him more determined to make contact with a Liberator.

"There has to be a way without the kitchen workers being involved. Targon, tell me all the people who are allowed through the kitchen and into the gardens."

"All of the gardeners, of course, the food pickers, who pick daily what is needed by the cooks and the Protectors."

"That's it?" asked Matt.

"That's it, I'm afraid."

"How do you know all this?"

"Because I've waited at the kitchen door for my mother on many occasions," said Targon.

"You've done what?"

"Waited for my mother at the end of her shift."

"And what pass do you need, to go into the kitchen and wait for her?" said Matt anxiously awaiting his answer.

"I don't. At first I used to show Protector 101 my ID tag, but after a while he got to know me and would just allow me through."

"Is it always Protector 101 at the kitchen entrance?"

"Usually, why?"

"That's it, don't you see?"

"No, I don't see."

"Targon, *you* have to go and meet Thera, not me!"

Chapter 6

Targon was looking remarkably fit, considering how seriously ill he had been. Dana collected two sets of fresh clothes from the laundry and tried to convince Matt that he couldn't stay in the same clothes for a third day. Matt studied the baggy blue pants and tunic hanging from the hook on the door and finally agreed that they were preferable to his blood stained jeans and jacket.

Targon laughed as Matt pulled the tight tunic over his head. "Now you look like me," he smiled.

"That's what I was afraid of," said Matt.

"I don't know how you can wear pants made out of such a coarse material. Ours are far more comfortable," said Targon, feeling the rough denim between his fingers.

Dana whipped them out of his hands. "I must hide these immediately," she said, folding them tightly.

Balder appeared in the doorway. "The Keeper is about to make an announcement over all screens in the Kingdom. Matt and Targon, you should listen to what he says. It sounds as though this is going to be important. I suggest you leave the door open a crack, but stay inside the room. We cannot risk you being seen by so many Workers."

Matt peered through the gap in the open door. He could see over one hundred people, all dressed in the same baggy pants and tunic tops, sitting at the tables under the glass dome. They were chattering excitedly and looking up expectantly at the large screen suspended from the central supports.

Protector 21 appeared at the top of the stairs and scanned the room. He took several steps forward and studied the various groups of Workers sitting at each table. His purple eyes shone brightly through the helmet visor and came to rest on Dorin. Balder shifted uncomfortably in his seat and hoped that Targon and Matt remained out of sight.

He nudged Dana. "Should I warn the boys that we have an unwelcome visitor?"

"No, it will draw attention to Dorin's room," she replied. "They are both well aware of the danger. I don't think they will do anything silly."

A fanfare of trumpets signaled the beginning of the announcement. Everyone rose, placed their right hand in the air and began to recite monotonously in unison.

"We, the people of the Kingdom of Zaul, thank the Keeper for our good health and prosperity. We are grateful for his protection and care, and we will continue to work hard for the benefit of the Kingdom. Bless the Keeper!"

"Good grief," whispered Matt to Targon, "do you really believe that stuff?"

Targon shook his head. "We recite the 'Oath to the Keeper' for fear of the consequences if we do not. I expect that you have noticed Protector 21 standing by the stairs?"

Matt nodded. Everyone sat down and the room went quiet. An image of an old man with balding head and long white beard materialized on the screen.

"My good people of Zaul. The enemy has attacked our defenses in the North and brought termination and destruction to many of your Protectors. Now we must fight back, and fight we will. It is imperative that we maintain the high rate of production of Xeleron. Any Worker in any sector who gives an additional two hours of labor will be given extra food rations. Emergency laboratories in Orange Sector will be opened for additional manufacture. Volunteers will proceed to these laboratories at the end of their regular shift. This means that our food production must also increase, and so must the production of weapons. It must be a united effort if we are to conquer the Kingdom of Prall. The Keeper blesses you all."

"Long live the Keeper!" shouted the workers as the image faded.

Satisfied with the response of the Workers, Protector 21 left the dome.

"Protectors do not like having to use the stairs," Targon laughed, "but seeing as we are not allowed near their magic boxes, they can hardly position them in our Sleeping Rooms!"

Balder, Dana and Norak walked back to Dorin's room.

"Well, that was no surprise," said Balder.

"No, the Keeper gets more and more greedy daily," agreed Dana. "We are no longer fighting the Pralls for land that was once rightfully ours, now we are trying to conquer their kingdom!"

"I think that the Workers have had enough. People cannot stand to work a fourteen hour shift," Norak said glumly. He closed Dorin's door firmly and sat on the bed between the two boys.

Matt sensed his despair. "The Keeper did say that it was voluntary. Perhaps everyone will continue to do twelve hours?"

Balder pulled up a chair. "Although the Keeper used the word 'voluntary,'" he explained, "what will happen is that the fourteen hour shift will come to be expected, until workers who continue with the twelve hour shift will be punished for not giving the extra time. Not so long ago we all worked eight hours a day. Look at us now!"

"Well then, it has become even more critical that we find the Liberators. Targon wants to try. Why won't you let him?" Matt pleaded.

"Because he no longer has an ID tag. If he were caught by a Protector without one, he would be terminated." Balder placed his head in his hands.

"There is something that I was hoping not to have to tell you," said Matt, "but it may change your decision. When I retrieved my CD-ROM from the Protector's Room I overheard a conversation between Protector 21 and three others."

"What about?" asked Balder.

"The Protectors are planning a rebellion. It will not be long before the Keeper is overthrown and all of the Commanders killed. The Cybergons want to rule the Kingdom of Zaul. Can you imagine what your lives would be like working for them?"

Balder flinched. "Are you sure about this?"

"Positive. I'm sorry, but I think it is a very real possibility, and we have to act as fast as possible."

"Well that settles it!" said Targon. "If you don't agree now, I will go anyway. Protector 101 knows me well, and I think the risk is minimal. Besides, you know as well as I do that I can't stay here."

"I think he's right," Dana reluctantly agreed. "The only worry I have is whether or not Protector 101 will have been informed about Targon's death?"

"We know from previous experience that it sometimes takes weeks before lists of the dead are distributed to the Protectors," said Norak. "Who knows if they ever read them anyway? 101 patrols the Red Sector. When have we ever seen him in Green Sector? I should think he takes little interest in the two hundred workers over here and probably only reads the lists of the dead in his own sector."

"I think you have a good point, Norak," answered Dana.

"Okay, we'll give it a try, but I can't say I'm totally happy about it." Balder drew in a deep breath and muttered, "I don't think Dorin will be very pleased either."

Targon got to his feet eagerly. "So, when do I go?"

Dana smiled at the boy's enthusiasm. "In the morning, Targon. You will have to go while we do our shift, since Thera will only pass by the kitchen entrance in the daylight. Dorin will escort you down the corridors as far as the kitchen and send you on your way."

"Great, I can't wait."

"That gives you another few hours to rest. I just hope

that you are well enough!" said Dana.

"Don't worry. I've enough energy to run from the Protectors!"

"You may need to," sighed Balder.

Chapter 7

Dorin was out of sight; Targon was on his own. He reached the end of Green Sector and turned left into the corridor where Red Sector began. One corridor looked like another. It was only through years of living in Zaul that Targon had learned how to find his way. But then, that was the object of the design, to keep the Workers within the confines of the few corridors that made up their sector and lessen the possibility of any rebellion. Targon knew the corridors better than most. He was one of the few allowed to travel between sectors. He passed an identical flight of stairs up to Red Sector Sleeping Rooms and walked by the laundry. The heat from huge washers and dryers escaped into the corridor, and the smell of detergent was a pleasant change to the chemicals he was used to breathing in. Targon decided that it would be a preferable occupation even if a hot one. The entrance to the kitchen was not far ahead. The smells of food replaced those of soap.

Targon felt his heart quicken with every step. He paused at the entrance and prayed that Protector 101 would be standing on guard on the other side of the large door. Slowly he placed his hand on the doorplate and pushed hard. He was met with an Xeleray pointing at his face. Not daring to breathe, Targon followed the long silver shaft of the weapon slowly with his eyes, upward to face its owner.

"Protector 101," he stammered with relief.

"It is you, Worker Targon."

"Yes, Protector, Sir."

"Is it the day for you to see your mother?"

"Yes, Protector 101. I hope she is well."

"I saw her this morning, and she was fine."

"May I be permitted to wait for her, Protector, Sir?"

"You may wait in the usual place. Do not get in the way of the Kitchen Workers."

"You are very kind. Thank you Protector, Sir."

Protector 101 gave a gentle bow acknowledging Targon's thanks, and waved him through.

Targon's heart continued to race as he made his way through the kitchen to the door on the opposite side. He dared not look back, and he dared not run. Protector 101 seemed almost human at times.

The kitchen made Targon happy. It was the single place in Zaul that had windows to the outside world. The natural light streamed into the room through large pains of glass. Fragments of dust danced in the bands, which shone in streaks across the surfaces. Targon thought how nice it must be to work in such conditions even if the Protectors were still on guard.

The enormous kitchen catered for thousands. Rows of large wooden chopping boards, on which the produce from the gardens was prepared, filled the back half of the room. In front were dozens of deep steel sinks. Workers bent over eagerly scrubbing vegetables and passing them back to those who chopped. The gigantic ovens were located in an attached smaller room built to contain the heat.

Targon reached the narrow porch between the kitchen and the garden and stood out of sight. He wondered if on this occasion he dared to prop open the door, so as to see through. The kitchen was very busy. The sudden increase in the demand for food caused by the Keeper's offer of extra rations had caused panic. Several cooks were leaning over huge metal pans, sweating profusely as various ingredients were added. Others were making Wheatcake, rolling out the dough, pressing it into round patties and carrying them into the adjoining room to place in the huge ovens. Targon licked his lips. His appetite had returned, and he definitely felt well again.

The exterior kitchen door swung open, almost knocking Targon over. A Food Picker kicked it even wider before struggling through. His arms were stacked high with freshly picked green Lingoones. The door stayed open. Targon bent his head round to see the beauty on the other side. The lushness of the landscape and the bright afternoon sky drew him closer. He inched forward stepping slowly into the sunshine, yet still holding tightly to the doorframe with one hand.

"How could this be the same Kingdom?" he asked himself.

An attractive stone path divided the cultivated area in two. On one side a variety of vegetables were mature and being harvested. The varying shades of green leafy plants contrasted with bright reds and yellows. Fruits hanging daintily from tall slender bushes bordered the entire garden. Across the path gardeners cultivated a rich deep brown earth, tilling and hoeing until the soil was so fine that grains lifted from the surface and occasionally blew away in the breeze. Targon was so entranced that he almost missed a slender figure walking by.

"Wait," he whispered.

The woman turned. "You wanted something?" she asked.

Targon shook his head; the face was not the one he was looking for. He was becoming anxious. Time was ticking by. The shift would end soon, and then he would be forced to leave with his mother so that the Protectors did not get suspicious.

He turned his attention back to the garden. There were rows and rows of every vegetable imaginable and hundreds of gardeners working diligently in the sunshine. He looked back at the path, which wound its way down through the center of the garden, ending at his feet. Walking towards him was another female figure. Targon stood up tall as she approached, hopeful that this time it would be Thera. The face was familiar. Targon hurriedly made the appropriate sign with his right hand. The woman smiled and returned the symbol. Targon continued with the 'F' for freedom, and Thera approached.

A loud voice boomed through the kitchen, so loud that it was audible from where Targon was standing just outside the door.

"I demand an immediate inspection of this sector. We are searching for an intruder."

It was unmistakably the voice of Commander Z.

"What, this minute, Commander? Dinner is at a crucial stage of preparation," said Protector 101. "It may ruin the food if we have to stop."

"Do not argue with a superior, 101. Since when have you been concerned about what the Workers get to eat? Protector 21, Roll Call immediately," he bellowed.

"Yes, Commander." Protector 21 pulled out his computer list.

"Tell me 101, have there been any unusual visitors to the kitchens in the last few days?"

"No, Commander, Sir," replied Protector 101.

"How about children, boys specifically?"

"No one new, Commander, just the boy Targon who visits his mother regularly."

"Targon, did you say Targon?" Commander Z howled, his voice showing the extent of his anger.

"Why, yes, Sir." 101 was surprised. "He's here now."

"It cannot be Targon! Targon was disposed of two days ago," Z bellowed. "At least that is what I was told! Protector 21, cancel the Roll Call and search the kitchens for the boy Targon immediately. Find him, now!" yelled the Commander.

Targon began to shake uncontrollably.

"Is it you they are looking for?" Thera asked.

"It wasn't, but it is now," said Targon, not knowing quite

how to explain his situation in a hurry. "Will you please help me?"

"Come with me," Thera said, leading him quickly along a path around the outside of the building and out of sight of the Protectors.

"The Commander may still decide to have Roll Call, so I can't risk taking you to Varl. You must understand that if I am caught, I will not be able to help others like you."

"Yes, of course, but what do I do?"

"Follow this path along the edge of the garden and into the field beyond. Stay low in the tall wheat grass, and you will not be seen. Walk through several large fields to the edge of Zaul, where you will see a small hill. A twisted oak marks the entrance to a network of underground caves. Enter and call Varl's name. He will come to you."

"Thank you, Thera."

"You're welcome. Now hurry. I must return to my work before I'm missed."

"One more thing, Thera. There are others like me in Green Sector, Workers who have had enough of the Protectors and want freedom. I just thought you ought to know."

"Thank you, Targon. It will be useful for us to know that in the future. Now go, quickly!"

Targon tore down the path without looking back, as fast as his legs would go until he reached the edge of the field. He sunk into the wheat grass breathing heavily and realized that Dana had been right - he was not one hundred percent better. He would have normally been able to sprint that distance without feeling the slightest bit tired.

Today he had to rest.

Thera returned to the kitchen door and listened for the outcome of the search. The Commander was exceptionally angry. The kitchens had been turned upside down, and Targon had not been found.

"I trust that you checked the boy's ID tag before allowing him through?" Commander Z asked Protector 101.

"Of course, Sir, as always Commander, Sir," Protector 101 lied. He knew that he would become dysfunctional if it were ever found that he had not followed the strict regulations for kitchen access. Commander Z would immediately have him returned to the Cybergon Factory and used as parts for new Protectors. 101 decided that he enjoyed his job too much to let that happen, and after all, what harm could a boy like Targon have caused?

"Then how is it that I have the boy's ID tag in my possession?"

"I have no idea, Commander. The boy showed me his ID tag as he entered," Protector 101 lied again.

Half a dozen Protectors pushed past Thera and reported to the Commander that the boy could not be found in the gardens either. Commander Z flew into a violent rage. He banged his fist hard against the wall.

"Protector 21, tell me how a young boy can elude so many Cybergons? And we have still not located the intruder! I shall inform the Modification Room that adjustments need to be made to your systems."

Protector 21 did not like the threat of modifications to his systems and felt he had tolerated being treated in such a way for too long. His intelligence far outweighed that of the Commander. He studied the man and wondered if the other Commanders were as arrogant.

"I want Balder, Dana and Norak brought to me for questioning. How dare they lie to me!" said Commander Z.

"You do not want them terminated immediately, Commander?"

"All in good time, 21. Until we find the boy Targon and the intruder, those three workers are of more value to us alive."

"As you wish, Commander Sir."

21 watched Z go. It was time for change. The Protectors must plan to take control soon, and he would lead the rebellion. But he must choose his moment carefully.

Rested, Targon had caught his breath and now continued the long walk. It was colder outside than he had expected, but how wonderful it felt to have the wind on his face and sunshine on his skin. He breathed in deeply, smelling the fragrances of the countryside and all that it had to offer. For the first time ever, he really felt that it was good to be alive, and the realization of what he had missed all those years slowly dawned on him.

The gnarled oak tree was easy to spot, standing on its own, twisted and withered on the side of the hill. Targon stood underneath in awe, looking up at its rotting branches bearing so few leaves. It was dying slowly, precariously balanced with exposed roots clutching at the sparse soil. Targon felt his stomach. The tree could have been him working in the laboratory, desperate for sunshine and freedom from the daily torture of working for the Protectors. He wished he could find water for its roots and revive the wizened trunk.

Targon walked a little way around the side of the hill looking for the entrance to the caves, but none was visible. He recalled Thera's words and went back to the tree.

"Where is it?" he asked himself, studying the rising mound of earth.

"I'm sure she said that the tree marked the spot, and there is only one tree." He leaned against the trunk wondering what he should do. A tall clump of grass blew in the wind exposing a barren spot of earth surrounded by rocks at the base of the hill. Targon walked over to examine it more closely. A small entrance, about six feet in diameter and descending gently, was wonderfully concealed. Targon climbed inside, slipping slightly as the stones gave way beneath his feet, and followed the tunnel downwards. After several yards, when daylight was no longer visible, the passage opened out into an enormous cavern. Attached to the walls were several oil lamps, which flickered with the movement of air down the tunnel. Targon felt the rough surface of the walls, damp with moisture and colorful with the many elements present in the rock.

"Varl!" hollered Targon. The name echoed several times down the passageways, which led deeper into the caves. Targon stood back in surprise, as the sound of his voice repeated itself. He called again, mainly for the pleasure of hearing another echo, and then waited in the silence.

A figure appeared from the darkness. The short gray

hair shone under the glow of the lamps, and the pale green eyes that greeted him had reassuring warmth.

"I am Varl. Who is calling me?"

"My name is Targon. I am looking for the help of the Liberators. I have fled from the Kingdom of Zaul."

Varl smiled and held out his hand.

"I am the leader of the Liberators. Come with me, boy. You will be safe from the Protectors here."

Targon took hold of Varl's long fingers and followed him deeper into the Earth. After some distance the tunnel ended and Targon found himself in another large cavern. This time a blazing fire burned in the center, the smoke finding its way to the surface through numerous narrow cracks in the roof. The cave had been decorated with colorful cushions and soft feather mattresses placed evenly around the edge. Targon, having been used to bare white walls for so long, was surprised by the brilliance of the room. If this was freedom, he liked it already. Several children suddenly appeared and offered Targon food and drink. They disappeared just as quickly down one of many passageways, which led off from the central cavern.

"Have a seat, Targon," said Varl finding himself a comfortable cushion near the roaring flames. "You seem surprised that we have an underground city here. These caves are a complex network of passages and caverns that lead for miles. Now tell me how you found Thera."

Targon recounted the story of how he had nearly died from the fumes in the laboratory and how his friends had taken a great risk by hiding him. Varl nodded with interest until Targon mentioned Matt from the year 2010 with his computer and CD-ROM. Varl got to his feet and scratched his chin, listening intently as Targon explained how he had witnessed the Magic Box and seen the image of Thera in the garden.

Targon paused and studied the expression on Varl's face. "Somehow I don't think you believe me," he said.

"I have heard of these small computers," said Varl. "It is known among the educated Zauls that Humans once had access to very powerful technology and relied upon computers to do everything for them. Unfortunately, Humans became lazy and allowed the computers to virtually take over their lives. Now a handful of evil men, and the Cybergons they control, run our world these few centuries later. I believe that human technology in the year 2010 would allow this boy Matt to somehow travel forward in time to our year. However, for us to be characters in his Computer Game,. . . well, that is just a little too far-fetched!"

"So how do you explain that he knew so much about the Protectors and Liberators? And how was he able to pull up an image of Thera?"

"Computer technology, my boy. Perhaps he can see the different paths that history could take in the future and is able to choose our destiny. Perhaps he has been sent to help us destroy the Keeper and gain our freedom?"

"Do you really think so?" Targon asked excitedly.

"I don't know, but if this Matt can help us, I don't care why or how he is here," said Varl.

"But I have no way of getting back there now. The Protectors know that I am alive, and my friends are in danger for helping me. So there is no way I can take you to see Matt."

"Don't worry. The Liberators have been working for years towards the time when we might overthrow the Keeper and set the Workers free. There are over 1,000 who have joined our cause. Fifty Workers stay within the city walls to help us recruit more people daily, and the rest have found freedom here. We now have our own technology, which provides us with ways to get in and out of the city without being seen. We will go back tomorrow when you have regained your strength, and you will take me to meet this boy, Matt."

Chapter 8

Dana screamed. Protector 21 was pointing an Xeleray to her head.

"Get up, Worker Dana," he shouted, pulling her out of bed. 21 marched her to the door of her room and out into the central area. The sky was black, and the brightness of the nearly full moon lit up the room under the glass dome. At any other time, Dana would have stood and admired the beauty of the night sky. Balder and Norak were already there, both looking terrified with weapons aimed at them, encircled by Protectors.

"Workers, walk," commanded 21.

"Where are we going?" Balder asked.

"Speak only when you are spoken to," said Protector 21, hitting him hard across the head with the handle of the Xeleray. Dana gasped and watched Balder stumble slightly, but he picked himself up and continued to walk in front of her.

Balder felt the blood drip from his forehead onto his nose, across his cheek and toward his mouth. The salty taste found its way onto his tongue, confirming that he was indeed in serious trouble.

Protector 21 led them to an empty room on the upper level. Dana was shoved down on the stone floor, Balder and Norak next to her. The familiar white walls encircled them. There were no chairs, no windows and only one small light in the corner.

"Commander Z will be in to question you shortly," said 21. He marched out and the door slid across, locking firmly behind.

There was silence. Dana could not stop shaking. Balder's head pounded from being struck with the Xeleray, and Norak had tears in his eyes.

"They must have caught Targon," said Norak sadly.

"Not necessarily," said Balder screwing up his forehead in pain.

"Why do you say that?" asked Dana.

"Think about it logically. If Targon had been caught, we would have been terminated immediately for hiding him and lying to the Protectors."

"What makes you think we will still won't be terminated?" asked Norak.

"Perhaps they know that Targon is alive but cannot find him. Perhaps they are assuming that we know where he is," said Balder, thinking through the options.

"And perhaps this is nothing to do with Targon, but about Matt," said Dana.

"I hope not. He is the Worker's only real chance of freedom. No matter what happens, we must not mention his name," said Balder.

The door opened and the demonstrative figure of Commander Z strutted in, followed closely by Protector 21 brandishing his Xeleray. The Commander walked up to Norak and kicked his shins brutally with the hard toes of his black boots.

Norak winced in pain but kept silent.

"Liars, all of you!" he shouted. "How dare you lie to your Protectors. You know the penalty is termination. Did you really think that you could get away with it?"

"Get away with what?" Dana asked innocently.

"Speak only when spoken to," screamed the Commander, taking off his black gloves and smacking Dana hard across the cheek with the back of his hand. Her face stung but she was too proud to let him see that it hurt.

"Worker Dana, what did you do with the boy Targon?"

"We disposed of his body in the correct manner, Commander, Sir," she answered softly.

"Worker Balder?"

"It is as Worker Dana describes. We placed Targon's body in the furnace and brought the ID tag to Protector 13, Commander."

"Then why have I just had news that the boy was in the kitchens?" the Commander screamed in Norak's face.

"I do not know, Commander. Maybe it was someone else?" Norak answered.

"Someone else, when the boy was identified by Protector 101?" He continued to scream.

"Many boys look the same. Could he not have been mistaken, Commander? We have no reason to lie to you; we know the consequences well, and I am sure that you will hear from Protector 13 that we are good Workers and do not cause trouble," Balder bravely said.

Commander Z stepped backwards. "Then who might this other boy have been?"

"Did you not say you were looking for an intruder the other day?" said Dana. "Could he not have taken on the identity of Targon?"

The Commander turned towards Protector 21, standing silently behind.

"Perhaps she has a point. Maybe we are only searching for one boy and not two? Let them go."

Protector 21 made no move to release them. Instead he stood erect, armed his weapon and pointed it directly at the Commander's head. His purple eyes flashed through the visor in his helmet and shone on Commander Z.

"I think not, Commander," he said. "You are losing control. I, Protector 21, will now command this sector."

Commander Z opened his mouth to issue another order, as if he hadn't quite grasped what Protector 21 was saying, but 21's Xeleray made a whirring sound before a word came out of the Commander's mouth. A bright blue ball of fire hit the Commander in the head, turning him into a pile of black ashes. Smoke rose from the floor. There was nothing left of the Commander.

Dana huddled up to Balder, not knowing whether to be thankful for the extermination of the Commander or frightened of Protector 21. It seemed that Matt from 2010 had been correct: This was the beginning of the rebellion of the Cybergons.

Protector 21 turned to face them and once again loaded his weapon by sliding the control on the side.

"A weak man," he said. "Emotions and thoughts lead to weakness. I am not so stupid. Do you think I believe your story? Well, you are wrong," he said and pointed the

Xeleray directly at Norak.

Dana shouted, "No, please, spare us!" but it was too late. The bright blue ball once again hit its target and Norak was no more. Dana wept, burying her head in Balder's tunic, not daring to look up at the penetrating purple eyes. If she were going to die, she did not want to see it coming.

The familiar metal click of the weapon being disarmed gave notice to Dana and Balder that for now the killing was over. Dana looked up and met the purple gaze. The light was almost blinding at such a close range but, she dared not look away.

"Now you have something to think about," said 21. "Cybergons do not tolerate liars. I will be back to ask the same questions in twenty-four hours, but I will expect some different answers!"

The door slid across, and the room was still. Two piles of ashes still smoldered on the tiles, and two figures sat frightened in the corner.

Matt was pacing the floor anxiously when Dorin returned from his shift. Targon had left hours ago, and neither Dana, Balder or Norak had been to see him.

Dorin looked grim. "Bad news, I'm afraid."

"They've captured Targon?"

"No, worse. They've taken Dana, Balder and Norak for questioning. Several Workers saw them being led away from the Sleeping Rooms a few hours ago."

Matt's heart sank. He had not known Balder, Dana and Norak for long, but they had become his friends.

"Will they be eliminated?"

"I have no idea. It is usual for workers to be eliminated on the spot, not led away and held for questioning."

"Do you think it is because of me?"

"No, because they would have come for me, too. I suspect it is to do with Targon."

"Great, just great," sighed Matt.

"I'm afraid there's more bad news."

"More? Isn't that enough?"

"It seems that your prediction may have come true. Several Workers say that Protector 21 has eliminated Commander Z and that 21 is now instructing all of the Cybergons to rebel and shoot their human Commanders."

"Gee, this is bad."

"I know. I don't know what we do next. Do we try to locate Dana, Balder and Norak, or do we wait and hope to hear from Targon?"

"We do neither. I'll open up the laptop and see if I can learn from the game instructions how to get to the Keeper. If we can obliterate him, maybe we can save our friends. It may be that we have no need to destroy him now."

"How do you work that out?" asked Dorin.

"If Protector 21 has taken over and wants the Cybergons to rule the Kingdom, won't he also have to eliminate the Keeper?"

"Good point, but then we will have the Protectors to deal with anyway."

"True, but I have a feeling that the Keeper is somehow the key to destroying the Cybergons."

"Let's get to work then," said Dorin.

Matt turned on his computer; he had been conserving

the battery and had figured out that he still had several hours left. He pulled up the menu and clicked on '**Rules**' once again. The list of options appeared on the screen, and Matt scanned down until he found number 9, '**The Keeper**'. Dorin watched, still fascinated by the small black box and its capabilities. Eerie music resounded through the room; Matt hurriedly turned down the volume. Images of long dark tunnels and iron gates flashed before his eyes, and a foreboding voice echoed in the background.

"What is this place?" Dorin questioned.

"You don't have any idea?"

"Never seen anything like it before. It's not very welcoming, though."

"Pretty spooky, you mean," said Matt. "The voice is getting louder. I think we'll be given some instructions again."

"Well, I hope that they are as clear as last time," said Dorin.

An image of a solid wall filled the screen. Slowly the picture rotated to the left until it focused in on a small iron door. The voice grew louder still and erupted into an ominous cackle. The laughing ceased and a sinister voice spoke in whispers.

"Long dark tunnels lead you under the Kingdom,
You must travel there to gain your freedom.
The Keeper is under lock and key -
Be ready for a surprise, when you go to see.
He, who you think is an enemy, may not be.
This place holds a secret that you must learn,

Be ready to go, it is still your turn."

The tunnels disappeared, and a sharp image of gray-haired man with a reassuring smile appeared before the screen faded.

"Wow! What do you suppose that all meant?"

"I'm not sure, but I think we ought to memorize it," said Dorin.

"I'll just write it down."

"How can you? We are not allowed to have paper or pens. It has been that way for many years."

"With a computer, I have no need for that outdated equipment!" Matt laughed and pulled up Microsoft Word on the screen. "Watch," he said, clicking on '**New Document**.' He typed frantically, writing down the poem as fast as he could.

"Think carefully about the rhyme. The tunnels are obviously underground," said Dorin.

"But how do we get to them?" asked Matt.

"I wouldn't like to hazard a guess!" said Dorin, scratching his head and pacing the floor.

"The image of the gray-haired man might be important. Perhaps he can tell us where the tunnels are. But how do we find him?"

"Thera might know who he is," suggested Dorin.

"Agreed. But risking another trip to the gardens when the Protectors are on alert would be not only very dangerous, but stupid, if you ask me!"

"Then we'll have to come up with another way," said Dorin.

Chapter 9

Targon awoke to the smell of food drifting down one of the tunnels. He was ravenous. He looked around the cavern. The flames had died a little overnight, but the air was still warm, and the bright colors of the furnishings made him feel very happy. For the first time in years, he looked forward to the new day.

Varl appeared, dressed as a Worker in baggy coveralls and carrying a tray of hot toasted Wheatcake smothered in fruit sauce. Targon threw off the blanket and sat up eagerly on the edge of the feather mattress.

"Hungry, I presume?" Varl asked.

"You bet," said Targon, virtually grabbing the tray from his hands.

"Slow down, slow down! There's no hurry! I trust that you slept okay?"

"Just great, thanks," said Targon, stuffing down the Wheatcake. "You don't know how it feels not to have to worry about a Protector dragging you from your bed."

"Yes, I do," said Varl.

"You do?"

"Fifty years ago, as a boy, I lived in Green Sector, like you. The Keeper had been in control of the Kingdom for several years. The Commanders and Protectors had become very powerful. I decided that I couldn't carry on as a slave, living in fear of elimination for the rest of my life. And so, when an escape by a large group of Workers was planned, I joined them. For the last thirty years I have established a route to freedom for hundreds of Workers. Gradually we have built up a highly technical underground system, ready for the time when we could overthrow the Keeper and Commanders and control the Protectors. That time is nearly here."

Targon choked on his Wheatcake. "You're really serious, aren't you?"

"I am. Come, let me show you the fascinations of Varl's underground network!"

Targon shoved the final piece of breakfast into his mouth and followed Varl down one of the myriad tunnels. They took many twists and turns along the way. The passages were all brightly lit, but not with oil lamps as in the outer cave. Targon fingered the colored lights and ran his hands along the cables that joined them.

"We generate our own electricity," he said, sensing Targon's interest. "We have hot running water, ovens and toilets, and even a hot air system for the winter in parts of the cave complex."

"Unbelievable! How did this all happen?"

"Not easily, believe me. We started with virtually nothing and have worked steadily for years to accomplish what you are witnessing today."

"But how did you know how to build these things?"

"Many of the older men who led that first escape from Zaul remembered the time before the Keeper took control. Computers were accessible by all Humans, as well as Protectors. These men brought the computer technology with them. They taught the youngsters like myself how to read and write, recorded all they could for future generations and started the "Liberators" movement. Of course those men are now long gone. But we have carried on, determined that one day Zaul will return to being a free place for all. New Workers, like yourself, escape every day. The Commanders and Protectors seem unaware of the great rebellion that is bubbling under the surface."

"There is one thing that I didn't mention to you earlier. Matt from 2010 thinks that the Protectors are also planning a rebellion against the Commanders and the Keeper. He says it may happen soon," said Targon.

"It might be better for us if it did. At least then we are only fighting Cybergons, and not their evil human Commanders as well. Why not let them do some of the hard work for us?" Varl smiled at the thought and led Targon up to a steel wall, which totally blocked off the tunnel.

"What you are about to see will amaze you," said Varl, squeezing his hand between two rocks on a narrow ledge and flicking a switch.

"Step through," he said.

"Pardon?"

"Step through."

"How can I, when there is a steel door in the way?"

Targon asked.

"Watch," said Varl, and he strode through as if the wall were not there. Targon stood with his mouth open and then followed. He walked up to the steel sheet and placed a foot in front, expecting it to hit something hard. Instead, it disappeared through the other side, and his leg looked as though it had been amputated at the knee.

"Wow! How do you do that?" said Targon, finally joining Varl on the other side.

"Technology, my boy," he said with a laugh. "It is purely a projected image giving the illusion that there is a steel wall in front of you."

"Show me more, please!"

Targon turned around to see a room, unlike any cavern, full of people diligently working. It was a laboratory similar in size to the one Targon had left in Green Sector - only the atmosphere was cheerful and light, thanks to the numerous windows on the opposite walls. Targon looked at the brilliant blue sky and the craggy mountains beyond.

"Now that I know how good it feels to have the sun on my skin and the wind in my hair, I'll climb those mountains one day," he said walking closer to look out.

"I think you'll have trouble!" Varl laughed.

"Another projected image?" Targon asked.

"I'm afraid so. This room is really another cavern, but we have made it to feel more like home, wherever that may be."

"What are they all doing?" Targon asked, looking at hundreds of screens and monitors displaying writing and diagrams.

"The Liberators in here are working on many scientific projects which will be beneficial when we finally overthrow the Keeper. It is necessary for us to understand their computer system to gain entrance to all of the hundreds of corridors and rooms in Zaul. We also must understand how the Cybergons are programmed, and we must be able to neutralize the Xeleron that is stored."

"Xeleron stored? I thought we weren't making enough to keep up with the demands of the Kingdom's war with Prall?"

"Wrong. There is plenty. The Keeper is just anxious that should Zaul be attacked, there would not be enough to defend the Kingdom. Rightly so too. The Kingdom of Prall gets stronger every day. They hate the Keeper and want him overthrown as much as we do. Most of our supplies to build all of this equipment have come from Prall, and they will help us against the Protectors when the time is right."

"Will their Cybergons fight ours?"

"They do not have Cybergons. The people of Prall learned a lesson when they witnessed how Cybergons took over here in Zaul. Their Cybergons were all destroyed, and now all computer technology is carefully monitored."

"So they are friendly people?" asked Targon.

"Very," replied Varl. "At least twice a year a group of Liberators make the journey to Prall to exchange products and ideas."

"Isn't that a long way?"

"It takes several hours over the rugged terrain, but it is well worth the trip," smiled Varl. "There is plenty more to show you, but I think it is time that we went to see Matt, so it will have to wait. Are you ready?"

Varl led Targon back through the image of the steel door and into the tunnel system. A few feet into the passage, Varl began to climb a metal ladder, which was attached to the cave wall and disappeared between two overhanging rocks.

Targon followed close behind, grasping the rungs tightly and pulling himself higher. The ladder seemed to go on forever and he was beginning to tire, still not fully recovered from his fever. Clinging tightly to the metal bar, he looked down over his right arm. The tunnel floor had disappeared from sight and the thought of falling crossed his mind.

Finally, the narrow ladder ended. Targon pulled himself up on top of a rectangular platform alongside Varl. In front was another steel door like the one he had walked through down below.

"Let me guess, another projected image?" Targon laughed.

"Are you sure you want to go through with this? You realize that you are putting yourself in danger by going back into Zaul? We have many quick escape routes but have only just perfected the technology to combat the Xeleray."

"That's fine. My friends took a great risk for me. Now I have to return their help. Besides, my mother is also in Zaul, and I could not bear to think that I am enjoying freedom when she is still a slave."

"Right then. On the other side of this image is the store cupboard in the Cleanliness room in Green Sector," said Varl. "Of course we always take a risk that an armed Protector may be standing on the other side, but our hidden entrances are in places that are rarely frequented by Protectors."

"How do you stop the Protectors from walking through like we do?"

"This control switch disarms a force field. Except for the metal plates, which protect their essential systems, Cybergons are essentially computers covered in a thin plastic, skin-like veneer. Consequently, if one were to attempt to step through a force field, he would melt like an ice cube thrown into a glass of hot water. Of course, if you were to do the same without the field being neutralized you would receive a nasty burn." Targon trembled at the thought. "Don't worry, you can tell if the field has been deactivated. See this tiny red light?" said Varl, pointing to a small box on the wall. "You know it is safe to cross through when it turns green. I carry a remote so that I can rearm or disarm any of the force fields from the other side. Are you ready?"

Targon nodded and followed Varl through the projected door. The other side was all too familiar. Targon laughed when he found himself standing in the tiny dark closet, which stored mops and brooms. Varl opened the door slowly. They were lucky. The Cleanliness room was deserted. Targon shuddered at the starkness of the bathrooms and the lack of privacy offered.

"The number of times I have been in here and passed this closet . . .if only I'd known how close freedom was. Why haven't you rescued all the workers, if these doors to freedom exist?"

"Do you realize how many thousands of Workers there are?" Varl said. "The caves are already overcrowded, and it is hard enough taking in the one or two who find us every week. We would have nowhere to lead everyone to safety, so we have to wait for a time when we can destroy the Protectors and regain control of the Kingdom. Now, let's get out of here. Where am I likely to find Matt?" asked Varl, pressing the remote to reactivate the force field.

"In Dorin's room, Green Sector, next to the glass dome."

"Good. That's not far if I remember correctly. Your turn to lead," said Varl.

Matt was tired of thinking. He and Dorin had brain stormed several ideas but decided that all were too risky. They now sat in silence, each with a splitting headache.

A firm tap on the door brought Matt quickly to his feet. His heart began to pound. Had the Protectors come for Dorin, too? Dorin motioned Matt to hide in the small closet and took his time going to the door, composing himself first.

"It's me. Open the door," whispered Targon.

"Targon, my boy, come in quickly," said Dorin, relieved. Matt pushed his way out of the cramped closet, his face lifting when a familiar figure of an older man followed behind.

"This is Varl, leader of the Liberators," introduced Targon.

"We guessed," said Dorin, remembering the image of the gray haired man with the warm smile on Matt's computer screen. "So pleased you could come." Dorin rubbed his hands together in excitement. "Now, perhaps we can formulate some kind of plan. Sit down, both of you, and tell us everything."

"You won't believe where I have been!" said Targon excitedly. Targon recounted his travels, and Varl added information about the Liberators. Time was pressing on; Dorin had less than an hour before his shift began.

"Now, Matt from 2010, it is your turn to talk. Targon here seems to think that you have a great knowledge of both the Kingdom of Zaul and of computers."

"This whole scenario is actually on a CD-ROM I bought called '**Keeper of the Kingdom**,' and somehow I got sucked into my own game. Although I have a good knowledge of computers, I have no idea how I came to be here and no idea how to get back again. This all seems like a crazy nightmare. The only way I know how to survive is to play the scenario through, and find a way to eliminate the Keeper and free the Kingdom."

Varl scratched his head. "Well, I know that the majority of the Humans in the year 2010 were highly advanced technologically. I also understand the workings of computers and even some scientific principals that you probably don't understand. But - all of us, pawns in a child's computer game? That's just a little too unbelievable! If that is the case, why do you need me? Our fate is in your hands."

"Don't you see, your fate *was* in my hands, but I can no longer control events because I am now part of the game. I have tried to re-open the game and play the scenario out, but the computer won't reload a game that is already running. So, I am stuck in your world, and the only thing I can think of doing is to use the game information to physically play out the game and win!"

Varl shook his head and smacked his lips together. Matt wasn't sure whether that meant Varl didn't believe him or just didn't know what to do next.

"Will you join with us to fight the Keeper and the Protectors?" Dorin asked pleadingly.

"Seeing as that is what I'm already doing, and there seems to be some kind of incredibly twisted logic behind all of this, I don't see that I can refuse," smiled Varl.

Matt clapped his hands together with pleasure.

"I knew it! I knew that if we found Thera and the Liberators, we could move on with the next step."

"And just what is that?" Varl asked.

"See here," said Matt pulling up the rhyme from the Microsoft Word files. "This is our next clue, and at the moment Dorin and I have run out of ideas."

Varl read the poem aloud for the benefit of Targon. He stood up and walked round the room in silence.

"I know of these tunnels from when I was a child," he said.

"You do? That's great!" said Matt delighted.

"But the entrance was blocked up, or so we were told. Perhaps the Protectors now have another way in, operated by their computer system?"

"How do you think that their trap doors work?" asked Dorin.

"I'm not really certain, but I have thought for some time

that it may be a similar system to our projected images operated by the various terminals on the walls."

"If we could only find the Central Computer, we could perhaps download a virus somehow and put the terminals all through the Kingdom out of action," suggested Matt.

You're a clever one," beamed Varl. "I have often thought the same, but locating the Central Computer has been impossible."

"So, where do we go from here?" asked Matt.

"Well, I know where I'm going, and that's to the Laboratory!" said Dorin. "My shift starts in fifteen minutes, and I'm not about to draw attention to my sleeping room by not showing up for work when we are getting so close to freedom for us all. Besides, maybe someone has news of Balder, Dana and Norak."

"Agreed. You carry on as usual, Dorin," said Varl. "I'm going to take Targon and Matt back to the caves and pull out some old maps I have. Hopefully, I'll be able to locate the original entrance to the tunnels that run under Zaul. Then maybe we can find a way to get in."

Chapter 10

Balder examined the sliding door. It was unlike anything he had seen in Green Sector, at least a foot thick judging by the frame, and probably made of solid steel. Dana still sat huddled in the corner, staring blankly at the pile of black ashes, the death of Norak weighing heavily on her mind.

"Dana, we have to be strong," said Balder, walking over to comfort her. "Protector 21 hates weakness. He even said so. We have to stick to our story; it is our best hope of staying alive."

"How do you work that out?" Dana mumbled. "It didn't help Norak."

"Protector 21 needs information. He figured that by killing Norak, we would be frightened enough to relent and tell him what he needs to know."

"Maybe that's what we should do!"

"Dana, you're not thinking. What do you think he'll do to us if we tell him about Targon? Probably eliminate us for being liars and traitors."

"Perhaps. I suddenly don't care. We'll die whatever."

"Then do it for Norak. Do you think he would want us to

sit back and take the same punishment? No, we fight on for freedom!"

The door slid open. Protector 21 marched in, seeming in a slightly happier disposition. Behind him followed another Protector that neither Dana nor Balder had seen before.

"The rebellion has been successful. All commanders have been annihilated; the Protectors are in control."

Dana looked at Balder with horror. How had a rebellion been so easy? What happened to the Keeper? She knew that she dare not ask these questions, but Protector 21 was obviously very pleased with himself. Perhaps flattery might help their cause?

Dana suddenly felt brave. "We are pleased, Protector 21. We did not like the Commanders and would rather work for the Protectors."

Balder looked at Dana with surprise, wondering what game she was playing. 21 stared at her for a moment, his purple eyes flickering as he took in what she had said.

"Is that so? And why is that?"

"Protectors have been treated unfairly by the Commanders, like the Workers. I am sure that the Protectors will be more just to those who serve them, and in return Workers will work harder for the good of the Kingdom."

Dana could not tell if her flattery had any effect. Protectors were not supposed to show human emotions, but on occasion she had seen glimmerings of anger and pride as she'd observed the Cybergons. Protector 21 stood in silence for a few seconds. Dana's heart pounded against her chest. He did not seem to be hostile.

"If that be the case, Worker Dana, tell me of Targon."

"I do not wish to have the punishment of Norak, Protector, Sir. I wish to serve you in the laboratory, but I honestly have nothing more I can tell you. It is as we have always said. Targon died, and we disposed of his body in incinerator 3. Then we brought Protector 13 Targon's ID tag. We know nothing else, and therefore can tell you nothing. I am sure that you would not want us to make up a story to please you?"

Protector 21 turned to face the Protector standing by the door.

"This is Protector 101 from Red Sector. He knew Targon well and saw him in the kitchen yesterday. He checked his ID tag. How do you account for that?"

Balder decided that it was his turn to make some flattering remarks. "You are very clever, Protector, Sir, but you also saw the ID tag belonging to Targon, so surely it must have been an imposter? Young boys all look alike to me; I find it very hard to distinguish between them. Perhaps some Protectors also have this problem?"

Protector 101 spoke up. "Although I checked his ID tag, 21, I cannot honestly say that I took the time to look at the boy carefully. I find it as Worker Balder says. Many of the young boys look alike."

Protector 21 stood silent again. "So be it. Your lives are spared for now. You will remain in this room for several more days, and I will continue with Roll Calls and make more inquiries. If I find you have lied to me, the consequences will be immediate. Do you understand?"

"Yes, Protector 21," said Dana, relaxing slightly.

"Thank you for sparing us, Protector, Sir," said Balder. "We will try to serve you well."

"Protector 101, as punishment for your negligence in checking the boy Targon more carefully, you are assigned to stand guard over Workers Balder and Dana. They are only to receive one meal a day."

"Yes, Protector 21," said 101.

"Get the Workers to sweep up the remains of Commander Z and Worker Norak."

"Yes, Protector 21."

Balder and Dana sighed with relief as 21 strutted through the sliding door. Dana's tactics had worked. Now they faced a new challenge. Protector 101 stood by the door. He had defended them, and Dana had to wonder why.

"Thank you, Protector 101, for supporting our story."

"You are welcome. I liked the boy Targon. I do not think he would cause harm."

Dana looked at Balder. She could not believe what she was hearing. This softer sounding Protector seemed almost human and showed signs of compassion. Could it be possible?

"I must get the suction machine to clean up the remains. I will be back shortly."

The room was quiet again. Dana hugged Balder.

"You were right!" she laughed.

"You were brilliant!" smiled Balder.

"What do you think of 101?" Dana asked.

"I'm not sure. It almost seems too good to be true.

When have we ever come across a caring Protector?"

"Never, I would say," said Dana.

"Exactly."

"So, what are you thinking?"

"That this might be a trap to get us to confide in 101. After all, we know that Protector 21 is clever enough to devise such a plan," said Balder. "Why else would 21 keep us locked up, with a guard standing inside the room and not on the other side of the door?"

"You may be right. Perhaps this nightmare isn't over yet?"

Chapter 11

Varl fingered through a tatty box full of rolled up pieces of paper. Matt still studied his new surroundings. The projected image entrances to the underground cave complex had been almost too much for him to comprehend. He wondered what Targon had made of it, with his lack of understanding of even the basic things. If it had been difficult for Matt, coming from the computer age, how hard must it have been for a boy who was frightened of magic boxes and could not read or write?

"This is what I was looking for," smiled Varl, unraveling several large sheets rolled up together and spreading one on top, across the workbench. The discoloration of the edges and several tears showed its age.

"Always knew I'd have a need for these someday," said Varl. "Never throw anything out, that's what I say! Targon, grab that end, would you, and hold it down."

Matt leaned over and studied the careful pencil plans.

"Wow, how old are these?" he asked.

"They date back to a time before the Keeper took over, and they were brought here by one of the older men during the first escape. I suppose that would make them over one hundred years old."

"Wow!" said Targon. "They are drawn so carefully."

"The man who gave them to me was an architect, and so everything should be drawn to scale. He was involved in the building of the new city defenses when the Kingdom was threatened by many of our neighbors. The number of Cybergons constructed and programmed was also dramatically increased to make the necessary patrols around the Kingdom's walls. That was the beginning of the end of a free Zaul. Several evil men saw an opportunity to control the kingdom and gain wealth through the suffering of everyone else. The Protectors became their means to take over."

"It is ironic then, that the Protectors have now eliminated them!" said Matt.

"Eventually, after many years, one family became more powerful, and so the head of the family became the Keeper of the Kingdom of Zaul."

"I wonder if the Keeper has been eliminated, too?" said Targon.

"That's a good question, and one I hope we'll find the answer to soon. Okay, let's take a close look. Here is Green Sector, and here's the Forbidden Hall and the Protector's Quarters running above," said Varl, following the rooms across the map with his index finger.

"And over here, joined by several corridors is Red Sector, with the kitchens and gardens behind," added Matt, "and Orange Sector, where the additional laboratories are. Where is the Xeleron Store, the Cybergon Modification Room and the Weapons Factory?"

"Right here at the end of the Forbidden Hall," said Varl.

This whole huge area is off limits to Workers and very heavily guarded by the Protectors. I wish we knew more about Xeleray production, but we don't."

"What are these areas here?" asked Targon, unable to read the printing.

"Blue Sector, Purple Sector, Yellow Sector and Black Sector," read Matt.

"Wow, I didn't know all of those places existed," said Targon astounded.

"The Kingdom of Zaul is actually quite large. The Sectors have always been operated as closed units in order to prevent a rebellion against the Protectors. The Workers in each sector have very little knowledge about anything going on anywhere else."

"There must be hundreds of Workers," said Matt.

"Thousands and thousands actually, making weapons, furniture, clothes - all the things you've taken for granted and never thought about where they came from."

"Could the workers outnumber the Protectors if all of the sectors were to join together?" asked Targon excitedly.

"Definitely. Probably several times over. But until we find a means to successfully battle the Xeleray, or a means to either reprogram or dysfunction the Protectors, thousands of Workers would die in any rebellion. That's what you saw us working on in the laboratories yesterday. We have just about perfected something called the Heatshield to combat the effects of the Xeleray, but we need to produce many more of them and perform a few more tests," smiled Varl triumphantly.

"So we need to find the tunnels then," said Matt, "and I

don't see any indication of them on this map, do you?"

"No, let's try one of the others," said Varl, unrolling the second and spreading it on top of the other.

"Here, look, what do you suppose these dotted lines are?" asked Matt.

"This could be what we're looking for," said Varl. "I had never realized that the tunnels were so extensive. According to this, they run practically the entire length of the Kingdom."

"Can you see where we might get in?" asked Targon eagerly.

"Well, they were originally built as an escape route in a time of war, so one would imagine that they must come out under the exterior walls of the Kingdom in at least one place," said Varl.

"Could this be it?" said Matt, pointing to a red mark at the end of one of the dotted lines.

"It could well be. Do you see any others?" Varl asked. "My eyesight is not what it used to be."

"I think there are two others – here and here," said Matt.

"Where's that?" asked Targon, getting very frustrated at not being able to understand the plans. "I do hope that someone will teach me to read when this is all over."

"I promise you, boy, that I'll teach you, whatever happens," said Varl, pleased by Targon's eagerness to learn.

"One tunnel looks like it comes out under the Forbidden Hall," said Matt continuing to study the maps.

"Too risky," said Varl. "The outside walls there, and along by the Weapons Factory, are very heavily patrolled.

We'd never be able to get inside, even if we didn't have to re-open the tunnel first."

"Okay, let's forget that. How about this one? It looks like it comes out at the rear of the kitchen."

"It could even start in the food cellar – the entrance is right by the kitchen door," said Targon.

"Well, that's very heavily guarded too, but it is nearer and we can get fairly close without being seen. I don't know how we'd get through the gardens with so many Protectors on patrol," Varl thought out loud.

"I do," said Targon, pleased at last to be of some assistance. Varl and Matt turned to look at him.

"You do?" they said.

"At night! We know from Thera that the gardens are only open during the day. There is no night shift of gardeners!"

"You're right!" said Matt, delighted.

"Great thinking, Targon," said Varl, rolling up the maps. "That's settled then. We wait for dark and then take a look. I'll bring two other Liberators with us and collect some equipment together in the meantime."

Darkness fell suddenly in Zaul. The sun set within a matter of minutes. Targon leaned against the twisted oak watching the blaze of reds and pinks on the horizon descend out of sight. It was a moment that he wished he could hold on to forever.

"Okay, let's go," said Varl. "Targon, have you got the flashlights? Our homemade batteries are as powerful as those used to keep the Protectors functioning, so they should be more than adequate. Boys, meet Liberators

Gannis and Hebron. They're coming with us to carry some much needed equipment. Everyone ready?"

The small group set off across the fields of wheat. It was a pale moon, so there was enough light to see to walk and still remain under cover. A gentle breeze moved the wheat in ripples like a rolling sea, concealing the disturbance created by the human procession passing through.

At the edge of the kitchen gardens, searchlights scanned from above. They were checking for intruders from Prall, and for Liberators or Workers looking for routes to freedom. The party paused at the edge of the field.

Varl ran first to the rear of the kitchen, ducking the beams of light, while the others remained submerged beneath the tall wheat crop. He walked the length of the walls, staying close in their shadows, searching for a possible old entrance. He felt the brickwork, smoothing his hands over the surface, looking for a section where an entrance might have been plastered over. None was visible. It looked more likely that the door down to the cellar had to be the way into the start of the tunnel system.

Varl beckoned the others to follow. One by one, timing the passage of light across the gardens, they ran across the open space between field and garden to the relative safety of where Varl was waiting.

"I can't see any signs of bricked-up walls," whispered Varl. I think that Targon's guess that the tunnel may begin in the cellar is a good one," said Matt.

"What do you make of the door, Hebron?" asked Varl, fingering the surface. There was no sign of any lock or handle.

"The door is fairly traditional. Solid steel and not protected by any alarm system," said Hebron, examining it closely. "My guess is that the Protectors thought an alarm unnecessary, seeing that to enter the cellar a Worker would have to pass through the heavily guarded kitchens and into the gardens first."

"Well then, our luck is holding," said Varl.

Targon pushed against the door. There was no movement. "So how is it locked?" he asked.

"I would say that there is some form of digital mechanism within the steel," replied Hebron.

"Do you think that you can decipher the combination?"

"What am I here for if I can't do a simple task like that?" said Hebron, pulling out a digital decoder and placing it against the surface of the door. He put a headphone up to his ear and listened carefully, pressing various keys occasionally. "Done!" he said finally.

"Wow! I wouldn't mind one of those!" said Matt, impressed.

Varl pushed against the edge, and gently the heavy door swung free. He led the way down narrow concrete steps, slippery where they had been worn on the surface. The cellar was dark and disagreeably damp with a smell that reminded Matt of moldy mushrooms. Targon handed out flashlights and passed his beam across the inner two walls of the small room, highlighting rows of shelves filled with supplies.

"Don't see anything, do you?" he asked.

"No. . . but it won't be that wall because the kitchen is

the other side, so it has to be this one," said Varl, focusing on the longer of the two walls, directly in front of the steps. "I think we'll have to move a few of these crates and work our way across the shelves methodically."

Matt began shifting the slatted wooden boxes to one side. Targon followed with the flashlight studying the rough surface of the exposed wall.

"Nothing!" said Matt, bitterly disappointed.

"But there has to be," said Targon, determined. "You said that you could see indications of a tunnel on the map, so it just has to be here!"

"Okay, let's start again," said Varl, calmly. "Matt and Targon start with that wall, Hebron and Gannis work your way round from the other direction. This time take everything off the shelves and search right to floor level."

Targon started on the lowest shelf. He dislodged a large tub of wheat flour, which he had been reluctant to move before, and immediately noticed a change in the color of the plaster. "Look, Matt, what's this? Shine your beam a little lower."

"That's it. You've found it!" said Matt, moving more items as quickly as his hands would allow.

"Gannis, your turn," said Varl stepping out of the way. "Let us show young Matt from the year 2010 just what our technology can really do!"

Gannis, a young man with sleek shoulder-length hair, set to work. He produced a small instrument resembling a drill, with a clear cylindrical central chamber and a suction pipe attachment. Matt and Targon watched as the machine cast an orange glow on the surface of the wall. Without sound or mess, the plaster and red brick underneath seemed to magically disappear leaving a gaping hole big enough to crawl through.

"Wow, and just how do you do that?" Matt asked, more than interested.

"It is called 'accelerated particle decomposition,'" said Gannis, proudly displaying the cylinder now full of a fine red dust.

"And just what does that mean exactly?" asked Matt.

"Essentially we have the ability to reduce and break up some solid materials into almost microscopic particles and store them. We can also replace them again after with 'accelerated particle recomposition!'"

"So you mean that we can reconstruct this hole after we're through?" Targon asked, also intrigued.

"That's correct – and not a soul will ever know that we've been through."

"Wow!" said Matt again.

"Well, let's get going then," said Targon, eagerly peering through the opening.

The tunnel smelled musty, and there were no lights illuminating the way. It was sinister how the tunnels mirrored almost exactly those in Matt's computer game. The walls were built of small rectangular bricks. The damp and mildew made them seem several centuries old, resembling underground passages from before Matt's time. However, the relative symmetry of the brickwork suggested that they had been constructed in the last one hundred years.

After half an hour of following the same route, the group

came across a divide in the tunnel. Varl paused to study the map.

"Taking an estimate of how long we have been walking and the approximate scale of the map, I would say that we are here," said Varl. "That puts us directly under Green Sector. It would be my guess that the left fork would take us back towards the outer wall. If we take the right fork we should end up somewhere, two or even three floors, below the Protector's Quarters."

"Yes, I get the feeling that we are going deeper underground as we walk further," said Matt.

The boys followed Varl, shining their flashlights on either side, with Hebron and Gannis close behind.

"I expect us to come across some metal gates, too," said Matt. "At least, that was what was pictured in my game, and so far everything else has been eerily familiar."

A further turn in the tunnel brought the group face to face with a large wrought iron gate, just as Matt had described. He fingered the bars, wondering how they could pass through. It appeared to have no lock and no latch to the wall, yet it was definitely not a projected image. Matt attempted to shake the bars, but the gate remained firmly in place.

"Don't worry, boys," said Hebron producing another small machine from a plastic bag slung over his shoulder. He placed a flat end of a small black tube against a bar, and within ten seconds the metal had warmed and twisted in such a way as to provide a gap, and yet the bars were not hot to the touch. Hebron did the same to a second bar until the space between them was large enough to squeeze through.

"Don't tell me you can bend them back again easily, too!" said Matt, on the other side. Hebron smiled, as if to say, "Need you ask?"

The tunnel echoed with the noise of their footsteps plodding on deeper and deeper underground. The dank smell remained; fresh air was not entering the tunnel.

"If we are to find the Keeper down here, how could he possibly survive in this atmosphere?" Matt asked Varl.

"I agree. It is worse than the suffocating smells in the laboratory," added Targon.

"Perhaps the Keeper's rooms are accessible by computer controlled doors from the Forbidden Hall, or elsewhere in the Kingdom, like those you witnessed the Protectors using. The rooms are probably well ventilated and these tunnels are only an escape route for the Keeper," suggested Varl, continuing to lead the way.

The tunnel came to an abrupt end. In front stood a solid wall and to the left, a small metal door, similar to the one at the cellar entrance.

"What now?" asked Targon.

"Well, we don't seem to have a choice," said Varl. "I vote we try the door having come this far."

Hebron again took out his decoder, listening carefully to the sounds of the inner combination lock. A heavy clunk indicated that he had again been successful.

"So, are we ready then?" Varl asked.

"Well, I'm not turning back now!" said Matt.

Varl gave a gentle push against the door, and it glided open smoothly. Matt entered intrepidly, stepping into the dark interior glowing with green, red and white flashing lights. It reminded him of a Christmas tree, its strings of bulbs blinking in a definite pattern. A gentle calming hum filled the air. Targon followed, feeling the wall by the door for signs of a light button. He touched the black rubbery circle, familiar in Green Sector, and pressed it gently. A hanging central light brightly illuminated the entire room, overpowering the smaller colored lights. The room was filled with a dozen tall electronic cabinets containing circuitry and keyboards. The boys stood in silent awe of their remarkable surroundings. They had located the Central Computer.

Chapter 12

"**W**ell, this is not quite what I had expected," Varl said chuckling. "This computer system hasn't been updated in years. I somehow assumed that the Keeper and Commanders would have progressed beyond this technology by now."

Hebron and Gannis placed their equipment on the floor and remained close to the door. Matt walked round the huge consoles studying the dials and switches, explaining to Targon the meaning of various printed words on the system. Most of the computer language was beyond Targon's understanding.

"Does this mean that you think we can work out how to download a virus to make the system inoperable?" Matt asked.

"It may be possible. We might be able to use your laptop and download a Terminal Emulator Program, because this Central Computer will not use the same computer language as your Windows 2010. Only then could we conceivably download a virus," explained Varl. "Let me study this system for a few minutes. Then we'll head back to the caves, and I'll see what I can do to create a virus."

Varl walked towards the main console and fingered a few of the switches and knobs. He found a keyboard in a large drawer under the main console, sat down on a small stool, and began entering a few commands. A few lights flickered on and off, but to the outsider he seemed to be playing a guessing game.

"Jackpot!" he said, entering a further few commands. "Not only does this system control all of the terminals and trap doors, but I can also see evidence that the Cybergons are programmed from here, too."

The mention of the word Cybergon sent chills down Targon's spine. He backed away and stood quietly next to Hebron and Gannis at the rear of the room.

"So, how would that be achieved when there are so many of them?" Matt asked, leaning over Varl's shoulder as he continued to type.

"I would guess that the Cybergons are reprogrammed when they make their daily visit to the Modification Room," replied Varl. "I have been told by some of the more recent Liberators that each Protector has to download his patrol information every twenty-four hours. I would imagine that new instructions are also programmed in during that time."

"So there would have to be a direct link between the Modification Room and this Central Computer, correct?" asked Matt.

"Correct. Each Cybergon must also have a port somewhere on its body through which the new programs are downloaded."

"Well, I've seen enough. Let's get out of here," said

Varl, pushing the stool to one side. "We'll formulate some kind of plan when we get back to the caves."

A high-pitched electrical tone caused them to stop and turn back to face the Central Computer. A large screen rose slowly from the floor directly in front of the main console. The overhead bulb went out, and the flickering colored lights on the central computer suddenly died. The room was black and silent.

Matt clutched Varl's sleeve in the dark. "What's happening?"

"No idea," replied Varl, concerned. "Targon, got a flashlight?"

Before Targon could answer, a solitary white beam lit the room as though they were in a movie theater. A recognizable image of an elderly man with long white beard appeared on the screen.

Targon trembled and clutched Hebron's hand tightly. "It's the Keeper," he stuttered, raising his hand vertically in the air to honor the ruler of Zaul.

A deep voice echoed throughout the room. "Welcome, Liberators. I am the Keeper of the Kingdom. I knew that there would come a day when you would meet me face to face, and I have been prepared for your arrival."

"Where are you? Why do you not show yourself in person?" asked Varl. "This is not face to face. Surely the Keeper is not frightened of the Liberators?"

"The Keeper is not frightened of anyone."

"Then why do you not present yourself? Why must we talk to you from another room?" asked Varl.

"Silence! You Liberators can be tiresome. It is enough

for you to know that you will not be allowed to leave these tunnels."

"And why should the Keeper wish to hold us prisoner?" pressed Varl.

"You will not be kept prisoner. You will be eliminated!"

Targon let out a gasp.

"What have we done that we deserve such a penalty?" probed Varl, stalling for time.

"You are a threat to the stability of Zaul and to my authority as its leader."

"But a wise leader can see and feel the pain of his people," said Varl. "Do you not see the suffering of the Workers?"

"Everyone in Zaul has a purpose. Each of us exists for a reason. There is no suffering except when a Worker deviates from his purpose, and you have all deviated from yours!"

"It is a coward that kills another human without facing his enemy!" shouted Varl bravely. "What kind of man will not look his opponent in the eyes?"

There was silence. The face on the screen stared ahead, deep in thought. Varl wondered if he had pushed too hard. He half expected the Keeper to enter through a concealed entrance followed by several Protectors. Varl gently grasped Matt by the hand and inched backwards to the door.

The voice resumed. "Liberator, you are a clever one, but not clever enough. I will not be called a coward. I *am* looking my opponent in the eye."

"And how is that?" asked Varl. "It is merely a two

dimensional picture that looks me in the eye!"

The bearded elderly image on the screen flickered for a second. The lights grew brighter and the Keeper left the screen, transforming into a hologram, which stood on the floor directly in front of Varl. The old man smiled and extended his arm as if he had won a game.

"Does that now satisfy you Liberator?"

Varl laughed. "A two-dimensional image becomes a three dimensional image, but still an image nevertheless. How can that satisfy me? You still do not look me in the eye and are therefore a coward!"

The wizened face on the hologram turned angry. "The Keeper does not possess human form, and only uses this system when necessary to maintain the human image that the Workers have come to expect."

Matt gasped. "The Keeper is the Central Computer!"

"How right you are, young one. Indeed, a computer so efficient that Humans are no longer required to maintain my system. Do not let my old exterior fool you. I have the brilliant mind of the original human Keeper whose image you see before you. But he has long physically departed this world. He wanted to ensure that his control remained over the Kingdom of Zaul long after his death."

Varl made an effort to compose himself despite the great shock. He had to keep calm and think fast if they were to stay alive. He wondered how the Keeper would attempt to eliminate them and prevent their escape from the tunnels. The door remained slightly ajar. He must play along a little longer.

"How long have you been in control of Zaul?" Varl

asked.

"For so many years that the current Commanders have not met their human Keeper. They were told that the Keeper was ailing and did not want to be visited. They took their instructions daily via the terminals without question. And now I have complete control. The Protectors have been programmed to eliminate all Commanders, and the city of Zaul is now ruled by computers!"

"Not if we have anything to do with it!" said Targon angrily. He was suddenly more frightened by the thought of a becoming a lifelong slave to a computer than he was by the threat of elimination by the Keeper.

"You will not be able to stop me. It is already too late. By the time you reach the entrance to the tunnel you will be met by the Protectors that I am now instructing to find you."

"Of course, your single defect!" said Varl, antagonistically. "But that will take time. Only the Cybergons being reprogrammed in the shop right now will be able to follow your orders. You have no wireless Ethernet ability, and therefore you cannot immediately direct them all to find us - your one weakness!"

The eyes of the Keeper bulged like flourescent pink bubble gum being blown to bursting point. The pale skin of the old man turned to a network of protruding purple veins.

"Try to escape as you like, but the Protectors will hunt you down once they are reprogrammed and have received my instructions via the terminals. Several are already on their way. You will not escape me! Liberators will be destroyed!"

The hologram disappeared and the screen lowered

back into the floor, leaving Matt and Targon stunned and Varl quickly studying the plans.

"It's our only hope. There used to be another entrance here," pointed Varl. "If we can make it back to the fork in the tunnel, the left-hand passage should bring us out along the rear wall beyond the kitchens and near Red Sector laboratory. Hebron and Gannis, follow behind the boys, and we'll see if we can blow the ceiling in the main tunnel when we reach the fork."

Matt ran after Varl, surprised at the speed with which the elder man could negotiate the tunnel in the semi-darkness. Targon panted breathlessly. He was still regaining his strength, and the events since he had met Varl had exhausted his energy. Hebron kept urging him on from behind.

The group reached the fork. Echoes of several pairs of heavy boots resounded from the direction of the cellar.

"Several Cybergons have already been reprogrammed to find us. There will be more on the way within minutes," said Varl.

"Don't worry. I have good old-fashioned methods that will do an excellent job of delaying them," said Gannis, pushing a detonator into the plastic explosive. "Get going. I'll be behind with the timer. There'll be a thirty second delay. This should block off our route and prevent the Protectors from following."

"Hopefully their program won't tell them to search for another entrance!" Varl said.

The boys rushed ahead, listening for sounds of an explosion. Suddenly there was an almighty boom. Shock waves reverberated throughout the tunnel, shaking the ground beneath their feet. Rolling clouds of dust rushed towards them.

"I would say that was a success!" said Gannis catching up with the group.

"Well let's not take any chances. I won't be happy until we reach the safety of the cave system," responded Varl.

They reached the end of the tunnel. Another brick wall faced them. Patches of a different colored brick and mortar showed the signs that at one time there had been an entrance. Gannis removed the Accelerated Particle Decomposer from his bag and set to work in the same manner as he had in the cellar.

A solitary pair of boots could be heard in the distance staggering at a slow pace through the tunnel.

"Quick!" shouted Matt. "A Cybergon made it through."

"Hurry Gannis. You've got less than a minute before he rounds that last bend," said Varl.

"Believe me, I'm working as fast as I can!"

The wall in front disintegrated, leaving a clear-cut hole to the outside. Varl clambered through first and pulled the other members of his group into the open air. Gannis quickly closed up the entrance by using the tool in reverse. Matt sighed with relief. At least that was one Xeleray he wouldn't have to dodge today.

A hot bowl of soup revitalized their weary bodies. Matt sat on one of the colorful cushions, sipping away at the vegetable concoction, staring into the roaring flames of the pivotal fire. For once, the meal seemed pretty tasty, but perhaps he was just adjusting to the strange taste of the various foods?

Targon lay curled up on one of the feather mattresses. The ordeal had been too much for one who had been so near death only a few days previously.

Varl was quiet. He sat at a small table studying various old computer manuals and muttering to himself occasionally.   "I guess we can't risk downloading a virus into the Central Computer now," said Matt sadly. "We'll have to come up with another way to destroy the system. Getting back into those tunnels with the Protectors on alert will be virtually impossible."

The corners of Varl's lips curled upwards in a faint smile.

"I suspect you have an idea already," said Matt, slurping at the last few spoonfuls of soup.

Varl rose from his table and chuckled.   "But of course, my dear boy. You don't think I'm going to let the Keeper beat us now when we've come this far! No computer is ever going to control my life!"

"So, come on then, what's your plan? Don't leave me hanging," begged Matt.

"If we could capture a Cybergon and enter a virus through its port, we would be able to blow the whole system!"

"How's that?" said Targon sleepily, confused by the technological chatter that had awakened him.

"Because the very next time that the Cybergon visits the Modification Room and is plugged into the Central Computer System, the virus would automatically download and render everything inoperable," explained Varl.

"Wow, it certainly could work!" said Matt.

"**Would**, not **could**, my boy. We have just one very large problem."

"What's that?" asked Targon.

"Capturing a Cybergon without destroying it!" said Matt. "And if you ask me, I would say that is virtually impossible!"

Chapter 13

Protector 101 turned off the suction machine and placed it by the door. Dana sat silently in the corner and watched the Cybergon closely. His eyes were a lighter shade of purple than most of the other Protectors and his stance less threatening – or was she imagining it?

"Why do you stare at me, Worker Dana?" 101 asked.

"I'm sorry, Protector 101, but I couldn't help but wonder why you cleaned up the remains of Worker Norak and the Commander yourself, instead of making us do it as 21 had instructed?"

Balder flinched. Suddenly Dana had become incredibly bold, and he feared for her safety.

"Did you wish to clear up the remains?" Protector 101 asked.

"Not particularly, Protector, Sir," replied Dana, not understanding where his question was leading.

"Then it is as I had thought. I have watched you Humans display a bond between each other, and I did not think you would take any pleasure in disposing of Worker Norak's remains."

Balder sat upright, hardly daring to believe what he had heard.

"Now, Worker Balder, you look at me in the same strange manner."

"Forgive me, Protector 101, Sir," began Balder carefully, "but most Protectors do not seem to care what Humans think or feel, and instead seem to delight in inflicting pain and misery."

"I am sorry for that, Worker Balder, but I am not like many of the Cybergons."

"I cannot help but wonder if this is a ploy by Protector 21 to get information from us, when we really know nothing," said Balder, getting braver still.

"I can assure you it is not. Protector 21 is most displeased with me, and I must admit I do not hold a great respect for him or his methods. There was a time when Workers and Cybergons were not enemies, but worked side by side for the good of Zaul. I liked those times, and I liked the boy Targon."

"Forgive me for saying, Protector, Sir, but this is most unusual and rather hard for us to believe," said Dana.

"I understand. You are both good Workers, and I do not wish to see you eliminated. I would like to help you, but one Cybergon against thousands would be futile, and Protector 21 would send me to the Cybergon factory to be used as parts. I do not wish to become dysfunctional."

"Perhaps there is something you could do for us," said Balder, deciding that it would be a good test of loyalty.

"What is it you wish?"

"Could you get a message to our friend, Worker Dorin, in Green Sector? He will be most concerned about our disappearance, and it will make him very happy to know that we have not been eliminated."

"I must go to the Modification Room to download today's patrol information from my system. Protector 13 will relieve me for a short time. I will try to go to see Worker Dorin personally when I leave here."

"Thank you, Protector 101. You are most kind, and we thank you again for your compassion."

Protector 101 gave his usual tilt of the head to acknowledge the appreciation. The door slid open without warning, and Protector 13 marched in. 101's whole demeanor suddenly changed. He became aggressive towards the two captives, instructing 13 that they were to be watched carefully and not to be fed again.

"Do not let them escape before my return, 13, or you will have to answer to Protector 21." His purple eyes flashed a gaze in Dana's direction as he walked out.

Dorin lay on his bed, gazing at the ceiling, unable to sleep after his shift. None of the Workers had heard any more of Balder, Dana and Norak, and he now feared the worst. It had been over 24 hours since he last saw Matt, Targon and Varl, and the frustration of not knowing what they were doing was killing him. Dorin loved to be in the center of the action. Sitting on the sidelines annoyed him intensely.

There was a very precise knock on the door. Dorin leaped to his feet, anticipating the return of the boys. He hurriedly opened the door to be greeted instead by the face of a Protector staring down into his eyes. Dorin tried to recognize the golden numbers across the helmet. It was not a Protector that he was familiar with. Dorin's heart sank. Would he, too, now be eliminated?

"Worker Dorin?"

"Yes, Protector, Sir?" Dorin trembled.

"I am Protector 101. May I come in?"

Dorin hesitated. This was not a familiar tone used by Protectors, and he was totally bewildered by this visit. It flashed through his mind that perhaps his room was about to be searched. Matt had his laptop, and Dana had hidden Matt's bloody clothes. There was no evidence visible that Dorin could think of.

"Yes, certainly, Protector 101."

"This may seem strange to you, Worker Dorin, but I bring a message from your friends. Workers Dana and Balder wish for you to know that they are in good health and have been spared elimination."

Dorin's expression changed. The fear disappeared, and now utter confusion showed in the lines wrinkled across his brow.

"I can see that you do not believe me," said 101.

"It is not that I don't believe you - I am just accustomed to fearing Protectors, not being grateful to them."

"I understand, Worker Dorin. Your friends look at me with the same expression. I am not like the other Protectors; I do not enjoy purposeless elimination and destruction."

"Where are my friends?"

"They are being held in one of the rooms off the Forbidden Hall. Protector 21 has said that he will release them in a few days, but I cannot confirm that will be the case. Protector 21 will do as he pleases at the time."

"And what of my friend, Norak? You do not mention him."

"I regret that he is no more. His remains have now been disposed of."

Dorin felt tears creep into the corners of his eyes. Norak was a good man, and he would be missed.

"Thank you for the honest information, Protector 101. I am very grateful. Please send my best wishes back to my friends, and keep them hopeful of release."

"I will do my best to prevent them from being eliminated. Please give me something to take back to your friends as a sign that I did indeed pass on their message to you."

"But I have nothing to give you."

"Then, a message that will have meaning to them."

Dorin scratched his beard. "Just say that I am still playing the game from 2010."

"You are still playing the game from 2010," said Protector 101, repeating his words. "It is a strange message, but I will give it to them. Now I must return, or I will be missed."

Dorin opened the door just as twenty armed Protectors marched into the common area of the Sleeping Rooms and spread out around the wall under the glass dome. Protector 21 walked proudly into the common area dressed in a long purple cape, which he threw back over his shoulder. Dorin's heart skipped a beat, and he turned towards Protector 101, wondering if he was part of this raid.

"You must not let them know I am here," said 101, "or 21 will send me to the Cybergon factory."

Dorin was amazed. This was not what he had expected. Had he even detected a slight note of fear in 101's voice? Hiding a Protector from his own kind was unheard of, and they would both be in serious trouble if caught. Dorin studied the blue-clothed figure. He could only see the flash of purple eyes through the slit in 101's mask, but something told him that he should dig deep into his heart and help this particular Cybergon.

"Into this closet, quick," said Dorin, pointing to a small door at the side of the sink. Protectors never look in here because it seems too small. You will be uncomfortable, but it is deep enough to curl up in."

"I fear that I cannot bend into contortions like you Humans can, but I will try," said 101, squeezing himself into the narrow opening.

"Workers will enter the common area immediately," boomed the voice of 21.

Dorin walked out and hesitated in front of his door before taking a seat at one of the many tables in the center. It was usually the time that he slept after his night shift, so sitting in the bright sunshine beaming through the glass dome was an invigorating experience. The day seemed so beautiful outside. How could it be so awful inside?

"I am your new Commander-in-Chief," said 21. "The Cybergons are now in control of Zaul, and you will cooperate accordingly. Two hours ago, some of your kind attempted to eliminate the Keeper. This will not be tolerated."

Dorin drew in breath. This was almost certainly an attempt by Matt, Targon and Varl, but had they failed and been eliminated?

"We intend to capture the perpetrators and offer a reward of extra rations for anyone providing the names of the Workers involved."

Dorin felt a smile creep across his face. They had made it out again safely, even if they had failed to destroy the Keeper. There was silence in the room. Protector 21 walked between the tables studying the facial expressions of Workers who shifted nervously in their seats.

"Will no one talk?" 21 bellowed.

Still there was silence.

"Stand up!" shouted 21, pointing at a table of six Workers in the center. "Eliminate them!" he ordered.

Four protectors moved away from the wall. The Workers screamed and pleaded and tried to run. The whirring sound of several Xelerays penetrated the noise of the crowd. Several flashes of light, followed by a hail of blue balls shooting across the room, hit the helpless targets. Six piles of ashes lay on the floor. The sobbing of several women resounded in an otherwise silent room.

"So be it," said Protector 21, angrily. "If no one comes forward by tomorrow, six more will die! Protectors dismissed! Workers, clean up the remains!"

The room emptied as fast as it had filled; the Workers stunned by the tragedy disposed of the small piles of ash and then went silently back to their rooms. Dorin opened the small closet door and helped out the twisted frame of Protector 101.

"Thank you, Worker Dorin," he said, brushing himself off and straightening his helmet. "I fear that 21 will not stop this rampage until he finds his intruders. I am sorry for the deaths of those you care about."

"Thank you for your concern. I wish that the Protectors were all like you. Zaul would be a far better place if Cybergons and Humans could work together in harmony."

"Now it is I who become a traitor. I do not wish to work for 21. The Human Commanders were arrogant and greedy, thriving at the expense of your freedom, but 21 is beyond evil and must be stopped."

Dorin took a step backwards. "Are you saying what I think you are saying?" he asked.

"That I will help you in any way I can, yes."

Dorin felt like hugging the blue-clothed figure that showed so many human emotions, but instead he extended an arm and shook hands with the Cybergon.

"Now I must return to my post, or Protector 21 will become suspicious. I will find a way to free your friends, but then it will be up to you to get them out of Zaul. I will contact you again soon."

"Thank you, Protector 101. You have a heart and a conscience."

101 tilted his head in recognition of the appreciation and quietly left Green Sector.

Dana and Balder waited anxiously for the return of Protector 101. It had been several hours, longer than they had expected. Being trapped in the small, windowless room with Protector 13 enjoying their anguish made the time pass more slowly for them.

The metal door slid open. Protector 21 marched in. Dana studied his frame. He seemed to walk more and more like a Dictator, with an air of assertion and authority, every time she saw him.

"Where is Protector 101?"

"He had to visit the Modification Room to download, Protector 21," said 13.

"You will address me as Commander-in-Chief from now on, 13."

"Yes Sir, Commander-in-Chief, Sir."

Dana was amazed by this sudden superiority that 21 had adopted over the other Protectors. She looked at Balder to see the same surprised expression on his face. This Protector had taken the place of the Commanders and had placed himself in control. He was now an even more dangerous Cybergon.

Protector 101 entered the room. Dana and Balder sighed with relief.

"Protector 101 you have been away from your post for a lengthy period."

"I am sorry, 21, but downloading today's information took longer than anticipated. There was a slight problem with the port in my head mechanism."

"Apology accepted. You will address me as Commander-in-Chief in the future."

Protector 101 said nothing. Dana thought that this was another human characteristic appearing. 101 was obviously quite taken aback by the announcement.

"Did you hear what I said, 101?"

"Yes, Sir, Commander-in-Chief," said 101 hurriedly.

"Good. Now you and Protector 13 will eliminate these Humans. They are no longer of use to me, seeing as they were here during the recent attempt on the Keeper and obviously know nothing of the Liberators."

Balder's mouth dropped in disbelief.

"But you spared us, Commander-in-Chief, Sir," babbled Balder in a vain attempt to change the Commander's mind.

Emotionless, Protector 21 waved his gloved hand and opened the door.

"Eliminate them!" he said without looking back. The door slid closed. The room was silent again. Two vulnerable Humans faced two armed Cybergons.

Protector 13 armed his Xeleray; Protector 101 did the same. Dana and Balder begged for mercy and closed their eyes. The recognizable whirring noise began, followed by the bright flash of light. Dana held her breath and prepared to die, but there was no pain. She slowly opened her eyes. Balder still sat beside her. Protector 101 stood over a pile of ashes. He had turned traitor and eliminated Protector 13.

"Thank you for your mercy," Dana stuttered. Balder looked confused.   He was too much in shock to find any appropriate words of gratitude.

"Your friend helped me. Now I help you. Worker Dorin said to tell you that he is still playing the game from 2010."

"You really did go to see him then?" Dana asked.

"As promised. I did not go to the Modification Room to download my information because the information about my patrol and the fact that I am helping you would then be entered into the main system.   I would become dysfunctional. I want no part in this senseless elimination of Workers. This is not a good life for me. I am a slave to

Protector 21, as I was to the Commanders. I will help you try to escape."

Dana jumped to her feet. "I can hardly believe this is happening!"

"Where will you take us?" asked Balder, still a little distrustful.

"Back to your friend Dorin. He will find a way to get you out of Zaul. I somehow think that he already knows how."

"Perhaps you can come, too?" asked Dana. "You won't be able to stay here now."

"Perhaps. We shall see. We must go before it is discovered that these remains are not human and that 13 is missing," said 101 ushering a bewildered Balder to his feet. "I must pretend to take you as prisoners down the Forbidden Hall, so do not fear me if I act brutally towards you. If I do not act in that manner, I may be stopped and questioned. Let us hope that Protector 21 is occupied with finding the intruders and has left this sector."

Chapter 14

Varl had been in the Computer Lab all morning. Matt waited impatiently, tapping his hand on the lid of his laptop, and watching Targon learning to read a few words in a simple book that Varl found for him.

Varl emerged smiling, carrying a disc in one hand and some scrawled notes on recycled paper in the other.

"Okay boys, we have ourselves a virus!"

"Do you think it will work?" asked Matt.

"I don't have any doubts. Some of the greatest technological minds are working in the next cavern, and they have checked over everything."

"What does this virus thing do exactly?" asked Targon, putting down the ABC book.

"It will delete part of the memory that the Central Computer needs in order to run its own operating system. When the Central Computer tries to perform a simple operation, the program we download will have deleted the instructions, and the computer won't know what to do. It will then crash, eventually rendering all of the Cybergons and every terminal around the Kingdom inoperable."

"Wow!" said Targon. "You make it sound easy!"

"It is, if we can get the virus downloaded. Finding an easy Cybergon target is the hard part," explained Varl. "We have to attach a cable from Matt's laptop into the port, which I think will be in its head, to download the information. Then we must set the Cybergon back on its way without its realizing what we've done. Next, we will wait for it to visit the Modification Room."

"So then what happens?" asked Targon eagerly.

"When it downloads its daily information into the Central Computer, our virus will be downloaded too. The virus will not affect the Cybergon until it has been downloaded, because a Cybergon is collecting data, not trying to execute programs stored in his database. When any Cybergon returns to the Modification Room to receive its programming for the next day, there will be no new instructions received from the Central Computer. Within 24 hours, we should have thousands of Cybergons wandering the halls without purpose, harmless to the Workers." Varl clapped his hands together with pleasure.

"That all sounds just great, but where are we going to find an unarmed Cybergon?" asked Matt.

"Good question, and one I hope Dorin will be able to help with. I suggest we take all necessary tools and make a trip back to Green Sector before the start of the next shift. We have approximately four hours before Dorin will have to be back in the lab, so let's get moving. We will enter Green Sector the same way as before, through the projected image in the Cleanliness Room."

Dorin was still stunned—both by the visit from Protector

101 and by the massacre of six Workers ordered by Commander-in-Chief 21–when he heard yet another knock on his door. It had been a busy day, and he felt that he could hardly take anymore surprises. Wearily, he answered the door. The smiling faces of Targon and Matt on the other side were very welcome. Dorin embraced the boys and patted Varl on the back, virtually dragging them into his room with excitement.

"I'm so glad you're back. It has been killing me not knowing what's been going on, and I have so much to tell you."

"Not half as much as we have to tell you!" grinned Targon.

"I heard all about your adventures already," said Dorin.

"How?" asked Varl.

"Protector 21, now calling himself Commander-in-Chief, eliminated six Workers because no one would give him any information about the attempt on the Keeper. You can imagine how bad I felt watching them die when I knew that I was the only one in the room who could spare them."

"But you wouldn't have spared them by confessing, Dorin," said Varl. "Protector 21 would probably have killed them anyway, and you, too, just to scare any more Workers from joining the Liberators. Besides, by staying alive you now have a chance to free thousands."

"I suppose you're right; it was just so awful to watch. They were all so helpless."

"Well, hopefully those Workers will have given their lives for the freedom of the people of Zaul. Our big news is that we have found a way to destroy the Keeper."

"You have? That's great! What does he look like?"

Targon laughed. "It's not a 'he' but an 'it'."

"I'm sorry, I don't follow," said Dorin, totally confused.

"The Keeper is an enormous computer!" explained Matt.

"But it can't be! He speaks to all of us on the big screens."

"What you have been witnessing is an image of the original Keeper who was human," said Varl.   "He programmed the Central Computer before his death to use his thoughts and follow his plans for Zaul. However, the original Keeper didn't anticipate that the Central Computer would develop a mind of its own and destroy the Humans controlling the Protectors. Consequently, the Cybergons are now our masters, and Zaul is totally controlled by computers."

"This is all incredible. You are telling me that for years, we have all been serving a huge computer?" asked Dorin, sadly.

"I'm afraid that's just about it," replied Varl.

"So I hope that you are you planning on making another trip in order to destroy the Central Computer!" Dorin said.

"No, it is far too risky now that the Protectors know the route we took to get in."

"But you just said that you had found a way to destroy the Keeper."

"We have, but we need your help," said Varl.

Dorin stood up proudly.

"You do?" he said, surprised. He was not an educated man like Varl, nor did he have any knowledge of computers like Matt, but he had helped many Workers in the past. He was trustworthy and inventive. It felt good that they still needed him. At last he was in on the action.

"We need to find a way to capture an unarmed Protector so Matt can download a computer virus through its port. Once this is done, the Cybergon will pass the virus through the system and into the Central Computer when he makes his daily modification visit. The Central Computer will crash when it tries to perform the simplest of operations."

"Unbelievable. And you have this technology?" asked Dorin.

"Right here," said Matt, producing the disc.

"But as you can imagine," said Varl, "finding a Cybergon that is not accompanied by others - or armed - is going to be difficult. Then it would have to be taken to the Modification Room and hooked up to the Central Computer ports. We have some secret entrances from the tunnels near the Modification Room, but I need your input to locate a solitary Cybergon."

Dorin smiled. "I think that I may have a more preferable solution all round."

There was yet another gentle tap on Dorin's door.

"Dorin, it's us, let us in!"

"There's a Protector with them. It could be a trap," said Varl, spotting a flash of navy blue material through the little window at the side of the door.

"Don't panic. This is my solution," said Dorin, opening the door without a hint of fear. Varl and the boys moved out of vision from the door, not quite understanding Dorin's lack of concern.

"Welcome back," said Dorin throwing his arms round Dana and then shaking Protector 101 by the hand. "Varl, Matt, Targon, let me introduce you to Protector 101."

"He saved our lives and eliminated Protector 13," said Balder, seeing the fear written across Varl's face. "This is our friend, Protector 101, unlike any other Cybergon you will have come across. He will now be hunted by the other Protectors because of his actions."

101 tilted his head towards the boys and gave his usual nod of the head.

"I thank you for your kind words," he said. "Targon, I am pleased to see that it *was* you who came through my kitchens and that you are well. Now it is I who have the need to escape."

"I was hoping that you may be able to help us further," said Dorin.

"Zang it!" said Matt, realizing where Dorin's idea was heading. "We have no need to kidnap a Cybergon if Protector 101 will help us."

"I will be of any assistance I can," answered 101.

"We have a way to destroy the Central Computer, but we need a Cybergon to do it," Varl explained. "Once the Central Computer is put out of action, all the Cybergons will lose the ability to receive new programming. Within twenty-four hours, we will be able to control the Protectors to reprogram them for our own needs - or we could destroy them entirely," explained Varl. "Unfortunately, you will sacrifice yourself immediately because you will be hooked up to a port when the Central Computer receives the virus and crashes. The Central Computer will not be able to download a new program so you will become virtually dysfunctional."

"It is a lot that you ask of me," considered 101.

"We realize that, but your sacrifice will free so many," begged Varl.

"It is okay. I have no life here, and I would rather help the thousands of Workers than become dysfunctional without having been of any use."

"Thank you, Protector 101. I am just beginning to believe that I might win this game after all!" said Matt.

"Game? What game?" 101 asked.

"Matt was just joking, weren't you?" said Dorin scowling at him. "Believe me, this is all very real to us, and we need your help if we are to bring peace to Zaul and give freedom to future generations of Workers."

"Then tell me what I have to do," said 101.

"Where is your port?" asked Varl, producing a length of computer cable.

"Lift off my helmet. There is a hinged door in the back of my head."

Varl gently removed the shiny piece of metal, not knowing what would be underneath. Dana gasped. The Cybergon's head was made of smooth translucent plastic. Many red and blue wires resembling veins ran in all directions under the surface. The perfect oval had no features. The bright purple eyes shone in a rectangular glass band cut through the plastic shell. His mouth was but a small square plastic grid mounted on the surface. To the human eye he was quite ugly, and yet this Cybergon with his compassion and warmth had become a person in

Dana's heart.

Varl found a small hinged metal plate cut into the plastic at the rear of 101's head. The three-pronged plug inside matched perfectly with the cable that Varl had created based upon his observations of the Central Computer's wiring.

Matt plugged the other end of the cable into his laptop and installed the disc.

"Are you ready?" Varl asked.

"Go ahead. When the process is complete, I will make my way to the Modification Room and download the information," said Protector 101.

"Thank you, 101. You will never be forgotten, and the people of Zaul will remember you as a hero forever," said Dorin.

Balder shook 101's hand, and Dana kissed him lightly on the cheek. Had she not known better, she would have said that he even blushed, but seeing as he possessed wiring beneath his plastic surface and not blood vessels, it was not possible. Or was it?

Matt entered the necessary commands and watched as the program began downloading. Targon peered over Matt's shoulder as the little blue boxes slowly crept across the screen - 50% complete, 75% complete and finally 100%.

"That's it!" said Matt, closing the lid and removing the cable. "The virus has been downloaded. It is now up to 101."

"Good luck to you all. Know that I will do my best," 101 said, replacing his helmet. He left Dorin's room heading in the direction of the Modification Room.

"I hope he makes it," said Varl to the others. "According to our maps, the Modification Room is at the end of the Forbidden Hall. If it has been discovered that he has aided your escape, 101 may be eliminated before ever getting there."

"The thought crossed my mind, too," said Dorin, "but he is our best hope."

Chapter 15

A sense of foreboding filled the tiny room. For several days, every one of the people present had been caught up in the euphoria surrounding the arrival of Matt and the plan to eliminate the Keeper. Now that the chance of freedom was so close, the possibility of failure was hard to bear.

Varl studied the sullen expressions. Dana and Balder had lost a close friend, and their unpleasant experiences had made them realize that they could also follow the same fate. They would never accept slavery again. Targon had seen a better life. He had witnessed the beauty of what lay beyond the walls of Zaul, felt the sun on his skin and the wind in his hair. How could he ever go back to producing Xeleron? And Dorin? He was aging fast. He had witnessed and carried the pain of so many workers for years and years. He could do it no longer. He needed to end his life with a taste of freedom and a feeling that his efforts had been worthwhile. Varl's eyes fell on Matt. He was a strange one. Could they all really be players in his computer game, or was he some kind of time traveler from the beginning of the Millennium? Varl's scientific curiosity was aroused. Where the boy was from and how he came to be in Zaul should not matter if his objectives were the same as theirs. Indeed, Matt had worked relentlessly towards their freedom. However, Varl was a scientist first and foremost. He wanted to know the answers to his questions. Matt looked sad and depressed. Perhaps he really was trying to find a way back to Earth 2010?

Varl sensed the pessimism. It was time to formulate a plan and snap everyone out of the gloom that had descended since 101 left for the Modification Room. He unrolled one of the old maps across the corner table.

"Okay, everyone. I need your full attention," said Varl, enthusiastically. "We need to have an alternative strategy worked out. We cannot rely totally on 101 to destroy the Keeper. We are so close to freedom I can taste it. I will not allow us to fail now."

Matt was the first to his feet. "Just tell me what to do," he said eagerly. "The sooner we annihilate the Keeper the better, if you ask me!"

"Great. That's what I wanted to hear," said Varl. The others rose less fervently and gathered round the plans.

"So, Varl, what have you in mind?" asked Dorin.

Varl pointed on the map to a small room located at the end of the Forbidden Hall. "The Weapons Store," he said calmly. "This is the key to making our whole plan succeed."

"How is that?" asked Targon.

"Without Xeleron, the Xelerays are useless, and without Xelerays, the Protectors are also not much of a threat. We must destroy the supply of Xeleron!"

"That's not going to be easy," said Balder. "There's no

way to reach the Weapons Store without going through the Forbidden Hall."

"He's right," added Matt. "At one end of the Forbidden Hall is the staircase down to Green Sector and the door to the Protectors' Quarters, and at the other end is an arched entrance leading into a long corridor. That is where I landed when my computer crashed and I first arrived in Zaul. There were several doors off that corridor leading to the rooms you describe."

"And the Weapons Store is right next to the Modification Room," Dorin added. "So, that makes it even harder to enter without being seen. Protectors pass the Weapons Store to download their daily patrol information virtually every hour of the day. So, it's not as if there is a time period when the area is deserted."

"Not only that, we **want** the Cybergons to be visiting the Modification Room. If we used diversionary tactics so that one of us could enter, it would prevent the Cybergons from receiving the virus that 101 is hopefully passing into the system."

Varl stroked his chin with the tip of his index finger, staring at the plans in front of him. "There has to be a way."

"There is," said Dana, looking at Matt.

Matt's eyes lit up. "Of course, the Conveyor System!"

"Clever!" said Varl, delighted. "Now why didn't I think of that?"

"Can you do it again, Matt?" Dorin asked. "It means crawling even further this time."

"Sure, no problem."

"Balder, for what I have in mind, you would need to go too," said Varl.

"Count me in."

"But, before you all get too carried away, it's not going to be that easy! We know that a specific group of Protectors report on the hour, every hour to download information. I would imagine that we have as little as a five to ten minute gap between the departure of one hour's Cybergons and the new hour's arrivals."

"That doesn't give us long," said Balder less enthusiastically.

"I have no doubt that it will be quite dangerous," said Varl. "Do you still want to give it a try?"

"What exactly is involved?" Balder asked.

"Unfortunately we haven't yet developed a neutralizing agent, and seeing as Xeleron is a highly explosive material, there is no way that we can blow the lot up," said Varl. "I imagine that with such a vast quantity as is in that store room, we would destroy half of Zaul at the same time!"

"Wow," said Matt. "And all of us with it!"

"Precisely."

"So, how can we destroy the Xeleron without physically blowing it up?" asked Matt.

"I know," said Balder, smiling. "Dana and I have worked with the stuff for years. It becomes totally useless after an hour if it is not kept in the light."

"Exactly," said Varl. "You and Matt will have to remove the compelenoid chips from inside the controls of the lighting system. It is a quick but intricate job. It may take Matt's smaller fingers to remove the chips. You can practice on the Sleeping Room lights first. Hopefully, the Xeleron will be virtually inactive before any Protector enters the store room to re-stock his sector's supply."

"Great idea," said Balder. "I'll certainly give it a try."

"Sure," said Matt. "Anything to win this game!"

"You've got less than an hour. Dorin will have to sneak you into the conveyor shaft before the start of his shift. I'll demonstrate what you will have to do in a minute. Dorin, got any spare eating implements?"

Dorin produced a spoon and fork. "We're not allowed knives," he said, handing them to Varl.

"Then these will have to do. You'll need something sharp to use as a lever to remove the edge of the wall plate. The compelenoid chips are in a small box underneath."

Targon looked upset. "Can't I go?"

"No," replied Varl. "I have something just as important for you to do. I need you to leave immediately for the caves. Do you think that you can find your way along the tunnels?"

"Easier than along the corridors of Zaul, " said Targon, delighted to be included.

"Dana, you're to go with him," Varl instructed. "Find Hebron and Gannis and explain what we have done here. Get them to come back with as many Liberators as will volunteer and all the new Heatshield weapons. Aim to be back here for the end of Dorin's shift. That gives you a good eleven hours - plenty of time."

"Done," said Dana.

"We will need Hebron to meet us at the concealed entry

in the Cleanliness Room here in Green Sector," continued Varl. "Gannis must take a group to the projected image entry under the stairs by Green Sector lab. The door above, in the Forbidden Hall, leads to the Protectors' Quarters. We will need a large group of Liberators there, to prevent off-duty Cybergons joining their sectors or reaching the Weapons Store."

Matt shivered, remembering how he retrieved his CD-ROM from one of those rooms.

"After years of planning and waiting, now is the time to put our technology to the test," said Varl. "Let's get to work and set Zaul free!"

Protector 101 adjusted his helmet as he reached the bottom of the stairs from Green Sector Sleeping Rooms. He felt different inside and did not care that he would soon become dysfunctional. The thought that many Workers would remember his heroism on their behalf made him walk proudly along the corridor. He put his hand to his helmet, remembered the touch of Dana's lips on his cheek and visualized the smile on the boy Targon's face when he said that he would help them. These Workers had shown him more respect in the last few hours than any of his fellow Cybergons had ever done. The terminal by the laboratory door operated the nearest concealed entrance to take him above. 101 keyed in his code and stood on the marked green squares. Gently, as if floating on air, he rose upward, emerging at the end of the Forbidden Hall.

101 stepped onto the tiles and began walking determinedly down the length of the wide hallway.

"Put down your Xeleray," boomed the familiar voice of Commander-in-Chief 21 from behind. Several more Protectors appeared; they pointed their Xelerays directly at 101. 101 laid his weapon on the floor and stood still.

"You have some explaining to do!" shouted 21. "Where have you been, and where are Workers Balder and Dana?"

101 remained silent. He tried to think of a plausible reason for their disappearance but could think of none. His best hope was to play innocent.

"Answer me immediately!" screamed 21.

"I do not know where Workers Balder and Dana are, Commander-in-Chief, Sir."

"Were you not instructed to eliminate them?"

"Yes, Commander, Sir."

"So why is it that only one pile of ashes can be found in their holding cell? Those appear to be of a Cybergon and not a Human!"

"Protector 13 instructed me to visit the terminal and check for our next order, Commander, Sir. I left the holding cell, giving 13 the pleasure of eliminating the two Workers from Green Sector who had betrayed him."

"A good story," said Commander-in-Chief 21. "But not a likely one!" he snapped. "You have already witnessed my anger. I do not tolerate fools and traitors. Eliminate him!"

101 had failed. He looked at his boots waiting for the blast to hit and hoping that his Human friends would find another way to destroy the Central Computer.

"Wait, hold your fire!" hollered 21. "This is all too easy. Protector 101 is almost begging us to destroy him; he has presented no fight. He must contain information from his patrol that will help us locate the escaped Workers - perhaps even the Liberators. Take him to the Modification Room and download his information into the system."

If a Cybergon could ever smile, this would have been the moment. 101 felt a rush of joy surge through his system; perhaps he had not failed after all.

Chapter 16

Crawling along the conveyor system, it was hotter than Matt had remembered. Perhaps he had adjusted to the cooler temperatures of Zaul? It was only the domed areas that ever reached the temperatures that he was now experiencing. The lights in the shaft emitted a phenomenal heat and were very hard on the eyes. Balder struggled behind. It was not as easy for a large man to move in such a confined space. He followed without complaint, pausing at the white grids to breathe in the cooler air from above. Matt found it generally easier than before. His hand was almost better, and he had regained his strength, even if he had been surviving on Green Sector food for nearly a week.

There were few sounds from above. Occasionally a set of boots could be heard walking across the stone tiles. Matt and Balder would stop and wait until the Protector had passed by.

They reached a place that Matt remembered well. Balder peered upwards into the Protector's Quarters and took delight in eavesdropping on their conversation. Matt moved on quickly for fear that any slight sound they accidentally made would ruin the chances of a successful outcome to the whole plan.

With only a dozen grids allowing in cooler air from above, the long shaft under the Forbidden Hall was tedious and tiring. By the time that they reached the Weapons Store, Matt and Balder were exhausted and dripping with sweat.

The noise of many Protectors collecting Xeleron echoed down the shaft towards them long before they reached the final grid. Matt and Balder lay still between the metal rails listening intently as the numbers of Protectors in the room slowly decreased. It seemed that there was a distinct pattern of programmed behavior. The Protectors downloaded information and received new instructions in the Modification Room. Then they collected a new supply of Xeleron from the Weapons Store next door before returning to their Unit. Matt checked his watch. In five minutes, the room would be virtually empty and his job would begin. He fumbled in the front pocket of the baggy pants for the little silver key and began to loosen the four corner screws holding the grid in place.

Two separate Cybergon voices remained. Matt looked at his watch again; only eight minutes left before the next Sector would begin arriving. Protectors 464 and 422 seemed in no hurry to leave. Matt felt frustrated. *Come on, Come on, get out of there*, he thought. There was nothing he could do but sit and wait. If there were no time gap to get to the lighting system on this hour, he and

Balder would have to lie there for another sixty minutes and try again later.

The door finally closed and the room was silent.

"Right, let's go," whispered Balder.

Matt waited a further thirty seconds before removing the grid. "How long do we have?"

"Six and a half minutes," Balder replied.

"Think we can do it?" asked Matt.

"We'll have a go, and if not we'll get back into the shaft and wait another hour."

"I guess we can assume that either 101 has failed or that he has not yet downloaded the virus," said Matt. "Otherwise those Protectors would not have been collecting more Xeleron."

"They wouldn't have even known what the stuff was if the virus had taken effect," confirmed Balder, jumping out into the store room.

The brightness was almost blinding. The tubes of Xeleron remained in the transport crates, which were stacked in highly illuminated cabinets. Each cabinet contained at least fifty crates, protected by a glass door. Matt was aghast at the number of cabinets, which not only lined the walls, but formed partitions down the length of the room.

"It reminds me of the school library back home," he commented. "Except it's tubes of explosives on the shelves and not books!"

"Come on, Matt! Look for the wall plate."

"There it is, Balder," Matt whispered, pointing to a small white plaque at the far end of the room which blended in with the whitewashed walls.

"Right, let's have a go," said Balder, removing the spoon and fork from his pocket.

The familiar sound of a Protector's boots arrived outside in the corridor, and the door began to open. Horror struck, Matt tugged at Balder's sleeve. They quickly ducked behind the nearest aisle of Xeleron. Balder turned white as he felt the fork slip from his grasp. The door's shrill mechanism seemed to hide the ringing noise of the fork hitting the floor.

The Protector entered and walked to the nearest cabinet containing full Xeleron crates. Matt could see the fork on the floor at the end of the aisle. The shining prongs sparkled in the light cast from the nearest cabinet. Matt's heart thumped against his chest cavity. If the Protector noticed the fork, he and Balder were as good as dead. Matt stretched out the toe of his shoe and carefully dragged the fork, inch by inch along the tiles towards him. He tried to hide any sound by coordinating his movements with the noise made by the Protector removing the Xeleron from the cabinets. Finally the fork was within grabbing distance. Matt reached down and whipped it from the floor. Color returned to Balder's ghost-like face.

The Protector took two tubes of Xeleron and placed them in a loading bay attached to either side of the long barrel on his Xeleray. The empty tubes were replaced in a separate crate on a lower level. Carefully the cabinet door was closed, and the Protector turned and left the room.

"That was too close," said Matt, sweat glistening in tiny drops on his forehead. "How much time do we have left?"

Balder looked at his watch. "About three minutes now."

"Is it still worth a try?"

"How quick can your fingers work?" asked Balder, already removing the wall plate. The box underneath contained tiny gold and white compelenoid chips placed in a definite pattern, just as Varl had said. But there was a problem.

"The pattern's different," gasped Matt.

"Any ideas?" asked Balder.

"I can make an educated guess based on what I saw in the Sleeping Rooms. Dorin said the third one along in the top row would disconnect the lights and would be gold. The third one is white."

"Is the fourth one gold?"

"Yeah. It connects with the same one as the third should have done," said Matt.

"Do it!" said Balder. "Come on, quick. We only have two minutes before Protectors start the download process again."

Matt shoved his fingers between the tiny spaces in the box and wiggled at the tiny gold chip. It held steadfast.

Come on, budge, budge, thought Matt, getting thoroughly frustrated. "Quick, the fork," he said, virtually grabbing it out of Balder's hand.

Matt stuck the prongs of the fork under the edge of the chip. The fork was so wide it wedged itself under the third chip as well. There was nothing he could do. It was a case of remove both compelenoid chips, or neither.

"One minute left," said Balder. "Hurry it up!"

Matt twisted the fork back and forth with force until

suddenly two chips flew from the box. The room went black all except for a faint band of light, which shone from the conveyor shaft.

"Great! You've done it," whispered Balder. "Now let's get out of here!"

Chapter 17

Commander–in–Chief 21 boiled with rage. He had read the information from 101's patrol records as it downloaded. The names Dorin, Targon, Balder and Dana were firmly implanted in his circuitry. Varl sounded familiar, but he could not place him instantly. 21 drew up pictures from his memory of a young blonde boy who escaped Zaul years ago.

"A Liberator," he muttered angrily. "101 has been dealing with the Liberators! How dare he betray his own kind."

As for Matt, the patrol records indicated that this might be the intruder he was looking for. 21 could wait no longer. The rest of 101's records were relatively unimportant. He had the information he had been waiting for.

"Continue to download 101's records. I will look at them later," he instructed. Protectors 82 and 190 come with me immediately. I want these workers found."

The Commander-in-Chief could not reach the laboratory fast enough. He wished that he had the ability to run like he had seen so many Humans do over the years. He marched precisely and angrily along the Forbidden Hall, fuming that he had been betrayed.

"Check the laboratory for Worker Dorin. I want him and the others found. The Workers will pay heavily for this!"

21 followed the other Protectors through the heavy swing doors. The laboratory was in chaos. Several Workers were on the floor with Xeleron burns and the five armed Protectors were trying to restore order.

"What is going on here?" 21 bellowed, firing his Xeleray randomly into the air. The blue balls hit the ceiling and exploded. Workers ducked for cover beneath the metal worktops as large sections of roof plummeted to the ground.

The Commander quickly scoured the room looking for the familiar face of Dorin. His eyes fell on the Conveyor System. An elderly man ignored the fracas as he helped two figures climb out from the shaft.

"Welcome back," Dorin whispered to Matt and Balder.

"Yes, welcome one and all!" sneered 21, pointing an Xeleray at Dorin's back.

Matt and Balder froze. Dorin turned slowly round to look Commander-in-Chief 21 in the eyes. With the knowledge that 101 had succeeded and so had his friends, Dorin stood tall and proud and faced his enemy. The fear he once felt had gone.

"Eliminate me if you like, but I will never be your slave again. I will not continue to live this pathetic existence."

21 let out an evil laugh. The intonation in his voice made him sound like a depraved human.

"Elimination would be too easy. I would not dream of giving you the satisfaction of an easy death. No, I have much better planned for the three of you." 21 reached behind Dorin and pulled Matt out to the front by his hair. A handful of brown curls fell to the floor as the Commander released his gloved grip. Matt winced in pain but uttered no sound.

"So this is our intruder, the cause of all my problems! Nothing but a weak boy! So, tell me how you managed to elude my Units for so long?"

Matt refused to speak. He was not about to give 21 the gratification of any kind of explanation as to why the Protectors had failed to capture him.

"Have you nothing to say?" shouted 21. "Have you no fear of what will become of you all?"

Matt felt extreme anger mixed with unbearable sadness at being caught. They had nearly succeeded in setting Zaul free. Emotions swelled in the pit of his stomach and boiled to the surface. Matt spat at 21 and then let out a long raucous laugh.

Commander-in-Chief 21 seemed somewhat taken aback. This behavior had never been witnessed amongst Humans before. He did not know quite what to make of it.

He finally composed himself, straightening the purple jacket that once belonged to Commander Z. "Very well. You had your chance to speak. 82, 190, take them prisoner! We'll see if this smug expression is wiped off the boy's face when we find the others."

Something is wrong, thought Varl pacing back and forth in the Cleanliness room. It had now been nearly twelve hours since Dana and Targon had left for the caves.

Collecting together enough volunteers and all the equipment was not an easy task, but surely they should have been back long ago?

The door to the cleaning closet sprang open and Targon emerged, closely followed by Dana, Hebron and a small group of Liberators.

Varl's immediate joy at seeing them return turned to sadness. His disappointment was not easy to hide. "Is this all the Liberators who volunteered?"

Targon smiled. "No, don't worry, there are hundreds more on the way."

"And Gannis has already set off for the other entrance with around ninety volunteers," added Hebron.

"Great, that's more like it!" said Varl, perking up.

"So, what's the situation here?" Dana asked. "Any signs of Cybergon dysfunction?"

Varl shook his head. "Not that I have seen, but then, Protectors don't venture this way very often."

"Perhaps it will be noticeable at shift change?" suggested Hebron.

"I hope so, because otherwise we will have to start a rebellion. I am determined that there will be no more senseless elimination by Protectors. This is the day we reclaim Zaul!"

Targon was more than eager to begin. "So what are we waiting for?"

"I was hoping that Dorin would be back with Matt and Balder by now." Varl looked at his watch again. "The shift ended fifteen minutes ago. We'll give them five more and continue as planned without them."

"And what if something has gone wrong?" Dana asked timidly. "What if 101 didn't manage to download the virus, or if Matt and Balder didn't manage to destroy the Xeleron store?"

"Well then, we'll be facing thousands of Protectors instead of the few hundred who haven't yet been to the Modification Room," Varl answered, trying not to be too alarming.

Dana's face dropped. "Oh, and how will we possibly fight off that many?"

"Young woman," chuckled Varl, "have you not learned to put any faith in technology after what you have witnessed recently?"

"*I* sure have!" Targon laughed.

Varl took a Heatshield out of Hebron's hand and proudly displayed it in front of Dana. The shiny metallic disc held by an insulated strap resembled a saucer with several finger like projections radiating from the center. "These new Heatshield weapons have never been fully tested, but we believe they will work against the Protectors."

"And just how are they going to do that?" asked Dana skeptically, shuddering at the thought of facing hundreds of Cybergons.

"Our theory is that by melting the Cybergons' outer case, the heat will also penetrate the insulation that covers their wiring, causing them to fuse and burn out," explained Varl. "At the same time our weapon radiates a deflector shield. It will not only protect the user from the intense heat but will also emit a defensive barrier against the balls of Xeleray, sending them back towards the Protectors."

"It sounds too incredible," said Dana.

Targon grinned. "Yeah, but I bet it'll work."

"Oh, it will, I have no doubt. We've worked on these weapons for years," said Varl confidently.

"Even the Pralls have helped us by supplying materials for their production," added Hebron.

"Our only problem is that we don't have enough of them ready," Varl concluded.

Dana sighed. "So, Varl, what will we do if we're outnumbered?"

"I'm hoping that we can draw any unsuspecting group of Cybergons into our projected image entrances and so make up for the lack of weapons. As I explained to Targon, once we have passed through we can activate a force field. If a Protector were to attempt to follow us, his plastic coating would melt like an ice cube."

Dana sat on the floor. "This is all too much for me. The last few days, beginning with the appearance of Matt from 2010, have been like a dream. I keep having to pinch myself to prove that this whole thing is very real!"

"Well, I hope that your dream has a happy ending," Varl said, gently patting her on the hand. He looked at his watch. *Still no Matt and Balder,* he thought. *Not a good sign.* "Dana, I want you to stay here by the projected image entrance. As more Liberators arrive, direct them towards different sections of Green, Red and Blue Sectors in groups of about fifty."

"You're not waiting for Dorin then?" Dana asked.

"Sorry, but we can't delay this any longer. Gannis will be in position and expecting our arrival. Large numbers of

Liberators are on their way. We must overcome the Protectors as a combined effort around the Kingdom."

"Do I get a Heatshield?" Targon asked nervously.

"Sorry, but you've got another important job."

"What's that?" he asked, feeling somewhat relieved that he didn't have to face the Protectors.

"I need you to visit all the Sleeping Rooms. Warn everyone to stay in his room. The last thing we want is unsuspecting Workers getting caught in the crossfire."

"Done," said Targon eagerly.

"Oh, and Targon, then you come back here and wait with Dana. I don't want you wandering the corridors trying to see what's happening!" Targon didn't reply. Balder shook the boy by the shoulders.

"Promise me!" he shouted. "Or I will send you to the caves now!"

"Okay, I promise," said Targon reluctantly.

Dana lowered her head. "Be careful, Varl. Please set us free," she added as an afterthought.

"I'll do my best. Now you must promise me that you and Targon will stay put. If anything goes wrong, you head for the caves and activate the force field."

Dana nodded anxiously.

Varl felt like a General leading his troops into battle. He had never experienced war, but he knew that thousands of lives depended on his technology and leadership. An egocentric and a frightening thought.

He had waited for this day for years, planning and building, experimenting and testing. Now that it was here, he felt quite apprehensive. Perhaps his weaponry wasn't tested enough? Perhaps he should lead these good people back to the safety of the caves and spare them the horrors of battle? And wait another forty years? No, the Workers couldn't tolerate another year of this tortuous life, never mind another forty. It had to be today.

At the bottom of the stairs, Varl paused. He turned and looked back at all of the faces he had come to know. All the young men and women so eager to do battle and claim the Kingdom that rightfully belonged to them.

"Are we ready?" Varl shouted.

"Ready," they all cheered, waving the shields frantically in the air. Varl charged along the corridor, followed by the young Liberators still shouting excitedly. He would start with the Protectors in the laboratory.

The group had only advanced a hundred yards when the column came to a sudden halt. No one moved. After the loud joyous battle cries, the silence in the corridor was eerie. A group of at least sixty Protectors had descended the stairs and blocked the way forward, their weapons loaded but not raised. Commander-in-Chief 21 stood at the front using Matt, Balder and Dorin as human shields.

Varl's face dropped. He had not anticipated this event. The thought of having to kill his friends to get to the Protectors sickened him.

"Varl, I believe?" 21 said in a sinister tone. "I have been waiting a long time to meet the Liberators face to face."

Varl was thinking quickly. There was only one way that this Protector could know his name. Sheer delight twinkled in his eyes, and he became bolder for the knowledge of 101's success.

"And who is asking?"

21 became slightly agitated. "Commander-in-Chief, 21. Do you not see by my clothing?"

"I thought that Commanders were Human. Clothes do not make a Cybergon a man–or a Commander."

Hebron held his breath. Varl was being unusually courageous.

"You rile me, Liberator! No Worker would dare to be so insolent, particularly if the lives of his friends were at stake," said 21, prodding Dorin in the back with the shaft of the Xeleray.

"Friends? What friends? You mean these insignificant Workers?" Varl laughed. "These are three of thousands and can hardly be called my friends."

21 had a long way to go before he could fathom a man's reasoning. Although he had begun to show signs of human emotions, tactics were not part of a Cybergon's understanding. His anger was uncontrollable. The Commander pushed Matt roughly to one side and stepped in front of Dorin.

"Then try to tell me that you do not care what happens to the rest of the Liberators! I have seen Humans stick with their own kind."

Matt slowly edged towards Dorin and out of the center of the corridor. The Protectors behind him were entranced by the negotiations and unaware of his movement. Varl could see his friends nearing the base of the stairs. He continued even more boldly.

"Do you care what happens to the rest of the Protectors?" asked Varl.

"We are programmed to reach our objectives, and we will do what is necessary to attain them!"

"Even if you are destroyed in the process?" asked Varl.

"Humans have no weaponry capable of rendering us dysfunctional."

Varl felt exhilarated. It was time to put their new technology to the ultimate test.

"Is that right?" he asked confidently. "Liberators, are you ready? Set deflector shields!"

Matt quickly pushed Dorin onto the bottom step and, aided by Balder, helped him upward out of the line of fire.

21 was alarmed by the courage of the Liberators. Never had he encountered such opposition. The Protectors had always been in control.

"Eliminate them all!" he sneered, believing that this small problem would be rectified within seconds.

The front row of Liberators raised their Heatshields as a barrage of blue missiles thundered towards them. The whirring of the Xelerays was deafening. Matt watched as the first wave of Xeleron made a thunderous noise coming into contact with the heat projections given off by the shields. As if by magic, the blue spheres rebounded in the air and shot back at twice the speed towards their launchers. The Protectors seemed stunned as their ammunition headed directly back towards them. Within seconds, a dozen piles of ashes were visible in the corridor.

Commander-in-Chief 21 ordered a further attack, and several more Protectors came forward. A second wave of Xeleron flew down the corridor towards the Liberators. As on the first occasion, the fireballs rebounded towards the front row of Protectors and eliminated the senders.

Stunned by the Liberators' amazing defense, 21 screamed, "Where are the reinforcements?"

"I do not know, Commander, Sir," said Protector 42.

"Then, go and find out!"

42 climbed the stairs in a cumbersome manner, passing Matt and the others without even noticing their presence.

The Liberators waited for the next move of the Cybergons. Still blocking the corridor, they were in a perfect position to defend themselves, and the Heatshields seemed to be having the desired effect.

"Protectors 142, 254 and 39, forward attack!" 21 waved his arms vigorously and sent them marching down the corridor to fire their Xelerays at closer range.

Varl felt nervous. Would the Heatshields hold up to being fired upon at such a close range?

The first fiery blue Xeleron balls sped towards them and boomeranged as before, destroying 142 and 39. Protector 254 kept marching, closer and closer. He was now within thirty feet of the Liberators. The heat emitted from the Heatshields would not have any effect until the Cybergon was within fifteen feet of the weapon. If Xeleron were fired now, there would be fatal consequences. It was Varl's worst nightmare.

Two shots of Xeleron sped towards the Liberators. The Heatshields could not withstand the impact from such a close range. Three Liberators were eliminated. Protector 254 continued onwards, twenty-five feet, twenty feet, eighteen feet. Liberators moved in to fill the gaps left by those who were eliminated. They raised the shields and prepared themselves. 254 continued without fear.

"Now!" shouted Varl. "Turn up the heat emissions!"

There was a sudden smell of smoldering plastic, and black smoke circled in the air. Matt watched as 254 crumpled into a heap: a twisted, melted melange of wires and small metal pieces, the frame of a Cybergon now unrecognizable.

"Forward, attack!" bellowed Commander-in-Chief 21, enraged. He would not let these Humans take control of the Cybergons.

Ten Protectors marched towards them, slowing down at approximately the same distance as when 254 had launched the devastating Xeleron.

"They know our weakness," said Varl to Hebron. "We cannot survive an attack at a close range by so many!"

The voice of Gannis suddenly boomed down the corridor. "Protectors you are surrounded!" The moving column of Protectors halted and looked towards their Commander for further instructions.

21's eyes flashed to the open laboratory doors. He could not believe his eyes. Where did they all come from? Rows of Liberators lined the corridor behind the Protectors and were backed up even into Green Sector laboratory. Each carried a similar disc with the ominous finger like projections. He had been so preoccupied with Varl that he had failed to notice their arrival.

"Fight on!" 21 hollered. "Fight on, Protectors!"

There was utter confusion. Those Cybergons at the rear turned to face the Liberators directly behind, while the

Protectors in the front continued to fight Varl and his group.

Gannis and his men were so close to the rear lines of Protectors that the Heatshields worked instantly, shriveling the back row of Cybergons into small unrecognizable piles of wire and metal.

"These things actually work!" muttered Gannis, almost as if he couldn't believe it. His group continued at point blank range, using the Heatshields to attack rather than as a defensive weapon.

Gannis yelled down the corridor above the high-pitched whirring of the Xelerays. "Don't hold back, Varl. Attack, don't defend."

Varl had lost a further group of men. Gannis was right. He should not allow the Protectors to choose the optimum moment to fire their weapons. Instead a forward attack using the Heatshields as close range weapons of combat would eliminate the enemy before the Xelerays were fired.

"Turn up the heat emissions," shouted Varl. "Attack!"

Blue sparks flashed in the ceiling as a ball of Xeleron went awry. The corridor became pitch black. The lighting had fused.

Fighting continued in the dark, illuminated by the glowing heat from the Liberators' Shields and occasional bright blue flashes as Xeleron found a target. Varl shouted orders and encouragement to the dwindling numbers of Liberators. Acrid smells of melting plastic, combined with burning explosives, choked the Human lungs. Breathing in the confined space of the narrow corridor became difficult. It was impossible to estimate the casualties on each side. Balder, Dorin and Matt could only bury their noses in their clothes and remain hopeful in the limited protection of the stairs.

The noise faded until silence signified the end of hostilities. The small yellow lights flickered briefly and then provided a dim light as the emergency power system cut in. Matt was flabbergasted. The devastation was extreme. The corridor was void of Protectors except for small piles of blackened wiring and metal fragments, which served as a reminder of what had once been. The remaining Liberators were rasping in the smoky atmosphere.

Varl staggered towards the stairs. "You all okay?" he spluttered.

"Yeah, fine thanks," said Matt coughing. "At least, we will be when we get some fresh air."

"Good, then we'll continue. Hebron," Varl called out, "let's enter the Forbidden Hall and finish what we have started!"

There was no reply. Varl frantically hunted the remaining faces for his friend, but Hebron had become one of the many casualties of the battle. Part of the price of freedom, but hard to accept.

Varl choked back tears. "For Hebron and all the others who have given their lives, I will not fail to complete what we have begun!" he murmured bitterly.

Gannis appeared through the lifting haze. He patted Varl on the back. "A fair beginning—now let's have a great end!"

"I couldn't agree more. It should hopefully get easier," Varl said, optimistically. "With the virus downloaded and the Xeleron neutralized, our remaining task should meet less opposition."

"I presume that **Commander-in-Chief** 21 met a hot end?" Balder laughed as he cynically stressed the title.

Varl studied the positions of the numerous patches on the floor and said nothing. Dorin rose to his feet and stood alongside, looking at the pattern of cinder heaps and the various metal contents of each pile, and then at the close proximity of the stairs.

"You thinking what I'm thinking?" Varl asked.

"Do you think it's possible?" Dorin replied, looking him in the eye and fearing the answer.

"Zang it!" Balder interjected, catching their drift. "In the dark anything was possible."

Varl picked up his Heatshield. "Then we have to assume the worst. We may not have seen the last of 21."

Chapter 18

Dorin triumphantly climbed the spiral staircase and for the first time set foot in the Forbidden Hall. The sun welcomed him through the enormous arched roof.

"You described the Hall well," he said to Matt, taking in the strange angular architecture.

"Yeah, but the place has lost its horrific edge now that I'm not running from the Protectors."

"Not so fast, boy," said Varl. "The danger's not over. Keep back against the walls and away from the exits, both of you." Varl motioned the rest of the Liberators to pass by. They climbed the stairs and entered the Hall intrepidly, keeping Heatshields at the ready. Thirty had survived here, and how many in other Sectors? Would it be enough? Varl was concerned. It was quite possible that stray groups of armed functioning Protectors were still on patrol.

"Gannis, take a dozen men and head for the Protectors' Quarters. Be prepared for more opposition. We still haven't seen any sign of deactivated Cybergons."

"You're seriously worried, aren't you?" said Dorin.

"The place is just too quiet," replied Varl. "I don't like it!"

"I agree. There's something quite haunting about the atmosphere."

"Take cover. Activate Heatshields," Varl suddenly yelled, diving to the floor.

Two Protectors wandered into the Hall from the direction of the Weapons Store and Modification Room. Several more followed. Matt cowered behind one of the angular steel pillars, watching closely as the group approached. He felt the urge to climb to the top of the pillar for escape. But, there were no explosions or flashing Xeleron balls, no chemical smells or tumbling masonry. The Xelerays hung loosely by the Protectors' sides.

"Look at their eyes," whispered Matt. "There's no glaring purple light. It is almost as if they are brain dead."

"That's because they are," said Varl, standing to his feet and emerging from behind the pillar.

Dorin held his breath and remained hidden, watching as Varl boldly walked towards the nearest Cybergon. He stood directly in the Protector's vision and slowly removed the Xeleray from his hand. There was no resistance, no violent language—in fact, no recognition.

The Liberators followed Varl's example. Before long, a pile of Xelerays had built up in the corner, and dozens of Protectors were wandering around the Forbidden Hall, with no purpose and no ability to communicate.

"I think we can assume that 101 succeeded and that the Keeper is no longer functional," beamed Varl.

"I'll say! This is just the coolest thing I've seen," agreed Matt.

Balder found the courage to touch a Protector on the

helmet. "To think we were all so terrified of these!"

"Armed and programmed, they are very dangerous. Let's not forget that for the future of Zaul!" said Varl adamantly. "Right, let's make an inspection of all the rooms in Green Sector before moving on. Keep a lookout for Cybergons that haven't been deactivated."

"Just look for the purple eyes!" shuddered Matt.

Dana sat on the cold floor of the Cleanliness Room. It seemed hours since Varl had departed and the distant sounds of whirring Xelerays had drifted in their direction. Targon paced back and forth anxiously, occasionally stopping and peering down the corridor towards the Sleeping Rooms.

"I wish I knew what was happening," he said nervously.

"There's nothing you can do; you'll just have to be patient," said Dana firmly.

"I could go to the bottom of the stairs and see if there's any action by the laboratory?"

"You heard what Varl said, and you promised him that you'd stay with me. Don't go back on that promise now!"

"Okay, okay," said Targon, reluctantly. He was about to sit down next to Dana when a familiar sound reverberated through the corridor.

"Boots, I hear Protector's boots," said Targon alarmed, "coming this way!"

He dragged Dana to her feet in panic and backed towards the open closet door, which provided the cover for the projected image entrance. Dana clenched his right hand firmly. Targon held the force field activator tightly in his other. A lone figure was visible striding down the corridor, dressed in the ominous purple jacket and brandishing a Xeleray.

"It's 21," Targon stuttered. "And he's definitely not deactivated!"

"Then the Liberators failed," said Dana crushed. "What do we do?"

"We do what Varl said. Stay close to this door and get ready to use the force field."

Commander-in-Chief 21 approached in an unusually careful manner. He studied the two figures, his purple eyes flashing as he searched for any sign of the new technology displayed by the Liberators. Convinced that Dana and Targon were unarmed and easy targets, he moved closer and raised his Xeleray. They would make suitable hostages, and this time he would not be distracted.

"Worker Dana, you and the boy will come with me."

"We refuse," said Targon boldly, pulling Dana backwards over the threshold of the closet.

21 laughed loudly. The arrogance of the boy amused him. The bravery of the Liberators had been one thing, but now an unarmed boy was challenging his authority?

"And just how do you refuse? By backing into a closet?" 21 laughed again. "You *will* come with me," he reiterated.

21's words were lost in the voluminous sound of battle cries and charging bodies.

"Jump! Jump through!" shouted Varl to Dana and Targon.

The Commander turned in horror. Varl and the

remaining Liberators were racing towards him. He reached to grab Dana by the arm for protection, but his prospective hostages disappeared from view as if by magic. 21 stared into the empty closet in disbelief.

Varl and the Liberators halted at the entrance to the Cleanliness Room. "Surrender, 21. The Protectors are no longer in control."

"Protectors do not surrender. Humans will not dictate to me! I will regroup with Protectors from other Sectors."

"The Protectors of all Sectors are deactivated. You stand alone. The Keeper has been eliminated, and Zaul is now free from Cybergon control."

"You lie!" yelled 21. "Humans are not capable of overcoming Cybergon control. You attempt to trick me again!"

"Surrender or you will be eliminated!"

"If I surrender, you will escort me to the Modification Room. Eliminated or deactivated, they are the same to a Cybergon. You offer me no choice," 21 sneered.

Varl raised his Heatshield. Dorin, Balder and Matt arrived, pushing to the front of the group of Liberators to witness the proceedings.

21 studied the faces of his adversaries. "You have not won yet," he laughed. "Where there's a way out for two, there's a way out for three!" He plunged after Dana and Targon. The sizzling sound of burning plastic hissed from the closet.

Varl lowered his Heatshield. Everyone stood in silence. It was a fitting end for one so evil. The initial euphoria of reclaiming Zaul had gone, and an empty feeling remained in Varl's stomach. He turned to face Dorin and Balder.

"All freedom comes at a price. Let us not forget those that gave their lives today so that we can be free."

Dorin nodded. "I am sure that no one here will be able to forget. Now we have the enormous task of building a new Zaul."

Targon and Dana emerged through the projected image. They embraced Varl excitedly.

"I can hardly believe that we're free," said Dana, hugging Balder. "To be able to walk openly down the corridors of Zaul is something I've dreamed of."

"I know," replied Balder. It seems incredible to think that I shall not have to work or sleep in fear ever again."

"The first thing I'm going to do is find my mother and take a tour of the gardens!" said Targon excitedly.

"I think you're forgetting something," interrupted Dorin. He pointed at Matt who, feeling removed from the celebrations, had seated himself quietly in the corridor. "We owe a lot to that boy."

"So, what now, Matt from 2010?" Dorin asked, walking over and sitting on the floor next to him.

"Well, I definitely won the game!" he chuckled. "Now I have to find a way of getting back to my own time."

"I presume it's up to the CD-ROM thing?" asked Balder.

"Not exactly," smiled Matt. "I shall have to enter certain commands into the computer to conclude the game, and hopefully you will never see me again."

"But I will always remember you," interjected Targon. "And at least you will know that I am free to walk in the sun and get freckles too!"

Matt laughed. "You mean you want them?" he teased.

Dana clutched Balder's sleeve tightly. Another Cybergon was walking towards them. Unaware of its surroundings, it turned and took two steps backwards before heading forwards. Dana finally relaxed when the glaring purple eyes were not visible.

"Good grief – it's Protector 101!" shouted Dana running towards him. "Varl, Dorin, somebody help me!"

They sat 101 down in the corridor, leaning him gently against the wall.

"It seems so sad and unjust to leave him in this pitiful state, when he sacrificed his livelihood for our freedom," said Dana. "Can't you reprogram just one Cybergon?"

"I can do almost anything, my girl!" laughed Varl.

"As long as it is just *one* Cybergon!" said Dana shuddering.

Epilogue

Matt smiled. At last he was going home. His computer had gotten him into this mess, and his computer was about to get him out. Happy that he would never see another Cybergon in his entire life, he decided that after he arrived home, the place for *Keeper of the Kingdom* was in the trash. At least in *his* world, computers had not taken control of lives – not yet anyway.

"Did any of you ever believe me?" Matt asked.

Varl smiled. "Let's just say that I'm a scientist, and therefore I kept an open mind. Anything's possible."

Matt began to type in the commands to end the final scenario. Dorin and Targon watched anxiously.

The screen flickered and a familiar box appeared, blocking the images of battling Protectors and Liberators holding Heatshields.

WARNING-PROGRAM ERROR
This program has performed an illegal operation and
will be shut down immediately.
Anything not previously saved will be lost.
This program will restart automatically.

Horror swept across Matt's face.

"What does it say?" asked Dorin.

Matt was silent. The unthinkable had happened. He caught Varl's sad eyes. Varl understood the implications of what he had just read on the screen.

"Has the battery died?" asked Targon.

Matt shook his head. He couldn't find words. His heart began to beat violently.

The screen went blank for a second, and then the Windows 2010 logo reappeared. The computer began to scan its memory. The words **Keeper of the Kingdom** scrolled across the screen, complete with a fanfare of music. Matt prepared himself for the worst. He had been a **character** in the game, and not a player. Therefore, it had not been possible to save each step taken towards the final target of eliminating the Keeper. The whole nightmare was about to start all over again - but perhaps this time, Varl would be waiting for him?

"Halt, intruder! In the name of Zaul, the Protectors command you to surrender!"

Matt ignored the warning and continued to run. A vibrant blue ball of light flashed past his head. He fell to the ground and covered his ears as the shimmering sphere of Xeleron struck the wall and exploded with an almighty boom.

H. J. Ralles

H. J. Ralles was born in England but spent a portion of her childhood in the United States. She fell in love with the world of books and started to write stories at an early age. After graduating with a Bachelor's degree in Education, she enjoyed teaching creative writing to her elementary school pupils. With the arrival of her own children Ms. Ralles became a stay-at-home Mom but continued to write in her spare time.

In 1997, struggling to find books that appealed to her computer literate children, she rose to the challenge of producing a novel that would captivate them as much as their computer games. Keeper of the Kingdom is her first book. H. J. Ralles lives in the North Dallas area with her husband, two teenage sons and a devoted black Labrador.

ALSO BY H.J. RALLES

In 2120 AD, the barren surface of the moon is the only home that three generations of earth's survivors have ever known. Towns, called Daroks, protect inhabitants from the extreme lunar temperatures. But life is harsh. Hank Havard, a young scientist is secretly perfecting SH33, a drug that eliminates the body's need for water. When his First Quadrant laboratory is attacked, Hank saves his research onto memory card and runs from the enemy. Aided by Will, his teenage nephew, and Maddie, Will's computer-literate classmate, Hank must conceal SH33 from the dreaded Fourth Quadrant. But suddenly Will's life is in danger. Who can Hank trust - and is the enemy really closer to home?

Comments on Darok 9

"Darok 9 is a can't-put-it-down, go-away-and-let-me-read science fiction thriller, sure to please any reader of any age!" **Jo Rogers, *Myshelf.com***

"From the explosive opening chapter, the pace of Darok 9 never falters . . . Ralles holds us to the end in her tension filled-filled suspense." **JoAn Martin, *Review of Texas Books***

The Keeper Series Continues...

Keeper of the Realm

In 2540 AD, the peaceful Realm of Karn, three hundred feet below sea level, has been invaded by the evil Noxerans. This beautiful city has become a prison for the Karns who must obey Noxeran regulations or die at their hands. In the second thrilling story of the Keeper series, Matt uncovers the secrets of this underwater world. He must rid the Realm of the Noxerans and destroy the Keeper. But winning level two of his game, without obliterating Karn, looks to be an impossible task. Can Matt find the Keeper before it's too late for them all?

To be released 2003